My dear Rose,

I'm beginning to understand how the Snake works.
He exploits our deepest fears to instill darkness
in our hearts. Laudion was afraid of the dark. He
feared anything he did not understand—such as the
creatures of the night, the Globes. How do I fight
ignorance and intolerance?

I've always tried to resolve conflicts by talking with
and listening to others. I'm convinced that all of the
Snake's evil plots can be overcome when the souls in
the universe communicate.

But what would happen if even speech ever became
impossible?

The Little Prince

First American edition published in 2013 by Graphic Universe™.

Le Petit Prince ™

based on the masterpiece by Antoine de Saint-Exupéry

© 2013 LPPM

An animated series based on the novel *Le Petit Prince* by Antoine de Saint-Exupéry
Developed for television by Matthieu Delaporte, Alexandre de la Patellière, and Bertrand Gatignol
Directed by Pierre-Alain Chartier

© 2013 ÉDITIONS GLÉNAT

Copyright © 2013 by Lerner Publishing Group, Inc., for the current edition

Graphic Universe™
A division of Lerner Publishing Group, Inc.
241 First Avenue North
Minneapolis, MN 55401 U.S.A.

Website address: www.lernerbooks.com

Library of Congress Cataloging-in-Publication Data

Cappoccia, Héloïse.
   [Planète des Amicopes. English]
   The planet of the Overhearers / story by Héloïse Cappoccia ; design and illustrations by Élyum Studio; adaptation by Guillaume Dorison ; translation, Anne Collins Smith and Owen Smith. — 1st American ed.
      p.   cm. — (The little prince ; #07)
   ISBN 978-0-7613-8757-2 (lib. bdg. : alk. paper)
   1. Graphic novels. I. Dorison, Guillaume. II. Smith, Anne Collins. III. Smith, Owen (Owen M.)
IV. Saint-Exupéry, Antoine de, 1900—1944. Petit Prince. V. Élyum Studio. VI. Petit Prince (Television program) VII. Title.
PZ7.7.C365Pl 2013
741.5`944—dc23   2012028303

Manufactured in the United States of America
1 — DP — 12/31/12

THE NEW ADVENTURES
BASED ON THE MASTERPIECE BY ANTOINE DE SAINT-EXUPÉRY

The Little Prince

THE PLANET OF THE OVERHEARERS

Based on the animated series and an original story by Héloïse Cappoccia

Design: Élyum Studio
Story: Clotilde Bruneau
Artistic Direction: Didier Poli
Art: Diane Fayolle
Backgrounds: Jérôme Benoit
Coloring: Karine Lambin
Coloring (Flats): Jackyung Kim
Editing: Didier Poli
Editorial Consultant: Didier Convard

Translation: Anne and Owen Smith

Graphic Universe™ • Minneapolis • New York

★ THE LITTLE PRINCE

The Little Prince has extraordinary gifts. His sense of wonder allows him to discover what no one else can see. The Little Prince can communicate with all the beings in the universe, even the animals and plants. His powers grow over the course of his adventures.

The Prince's uniform:
When he transforms into the uniform of a prince, he is more agile and quick. When faced with difficult situations, the Little Prince also uses a sword that lets him sketch and bring to life anything from his imagination.

His sketchbook:
When he is not in his Prince's clothing, the Little Prince carries a sketchbook. When he blows on the pages, they take wing and form objects that he'll find very useful. Like his sword, it's powered by stardust collected on his travels.

★ FOX

A grouch, a trickster, and, so he says, interested only in his next meal, Fox is in reality the Little Prince's best friend. As such, he is always there to give him help but also just as much to help him to grow and to learn about the world.

★ THE SNAKE

Even though the Little Prince still does not know exactly why, there can be no doubt that the Snake has set his mind to plunging the entire universe into darkness! And to accomplish his goal, this malicious being is ready to use any form of deception. However, the Snake never takes action himself. He prefers to bring out the wickedness in those beings he has chosen to bite, tempting them to put their own worlds in danger.

★ THE GLOOMIES

When people who have been "bitten" by the Snake have completely destroyed their own planets, they become Gloomies, slaves to their Snake master. The Gloomies act as a group and carry out the Snake's most vile orders so he can get the better of the Little Prince!

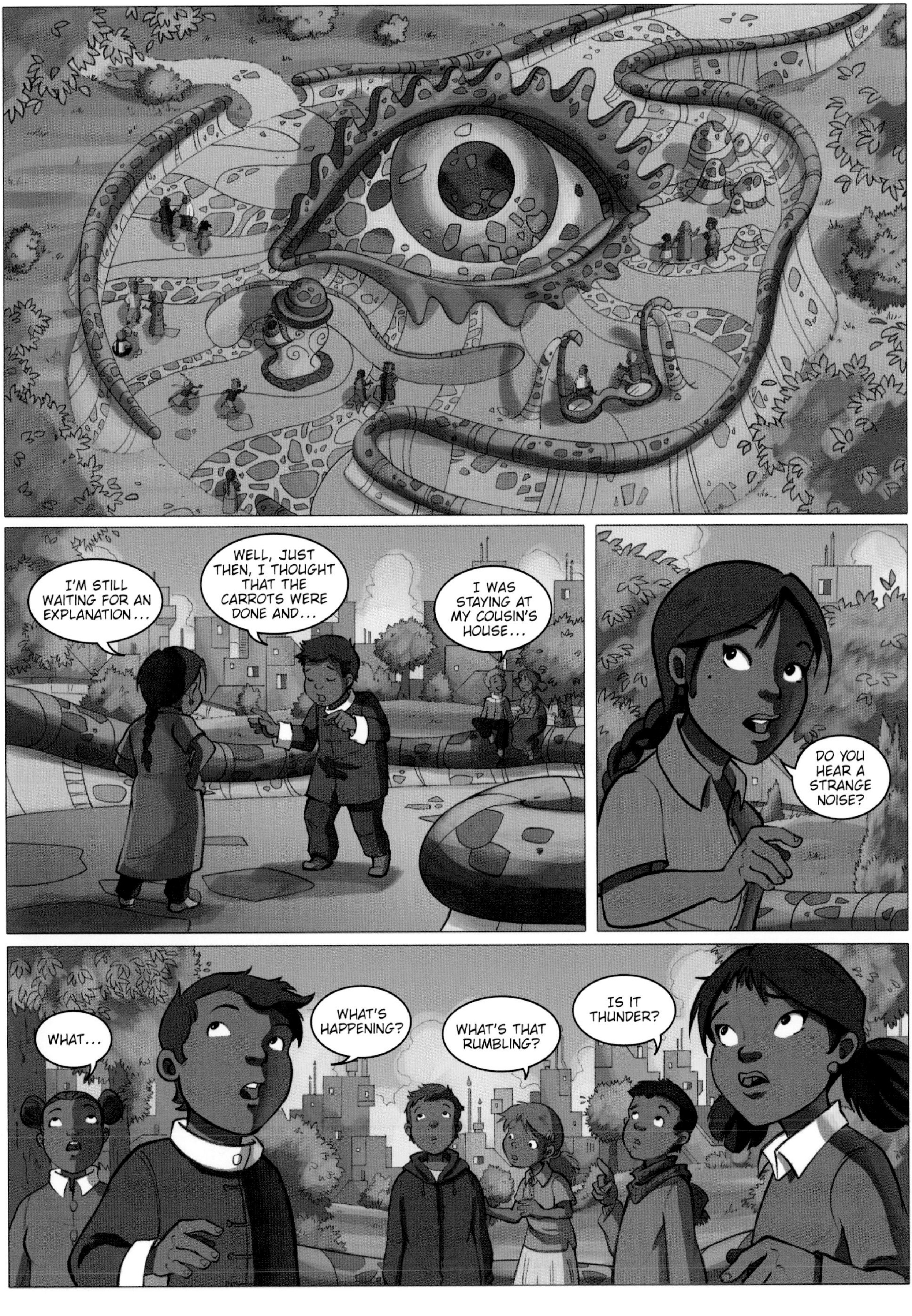
I'M STILL WAITING FOR AN EXPLANATION...
WELL, JUST THEN, I THOUGHT THAT THE CARROTS WERE DONE AND...
I WAS STAYING AT MY COUSIN'S HOUSE...
DO YOU HEAR A STRANGE NOISE?
WHAT...
WHAT'S HAPPENING?
WHAT'S THAT RUMBLING?
IS IT THUNDER?

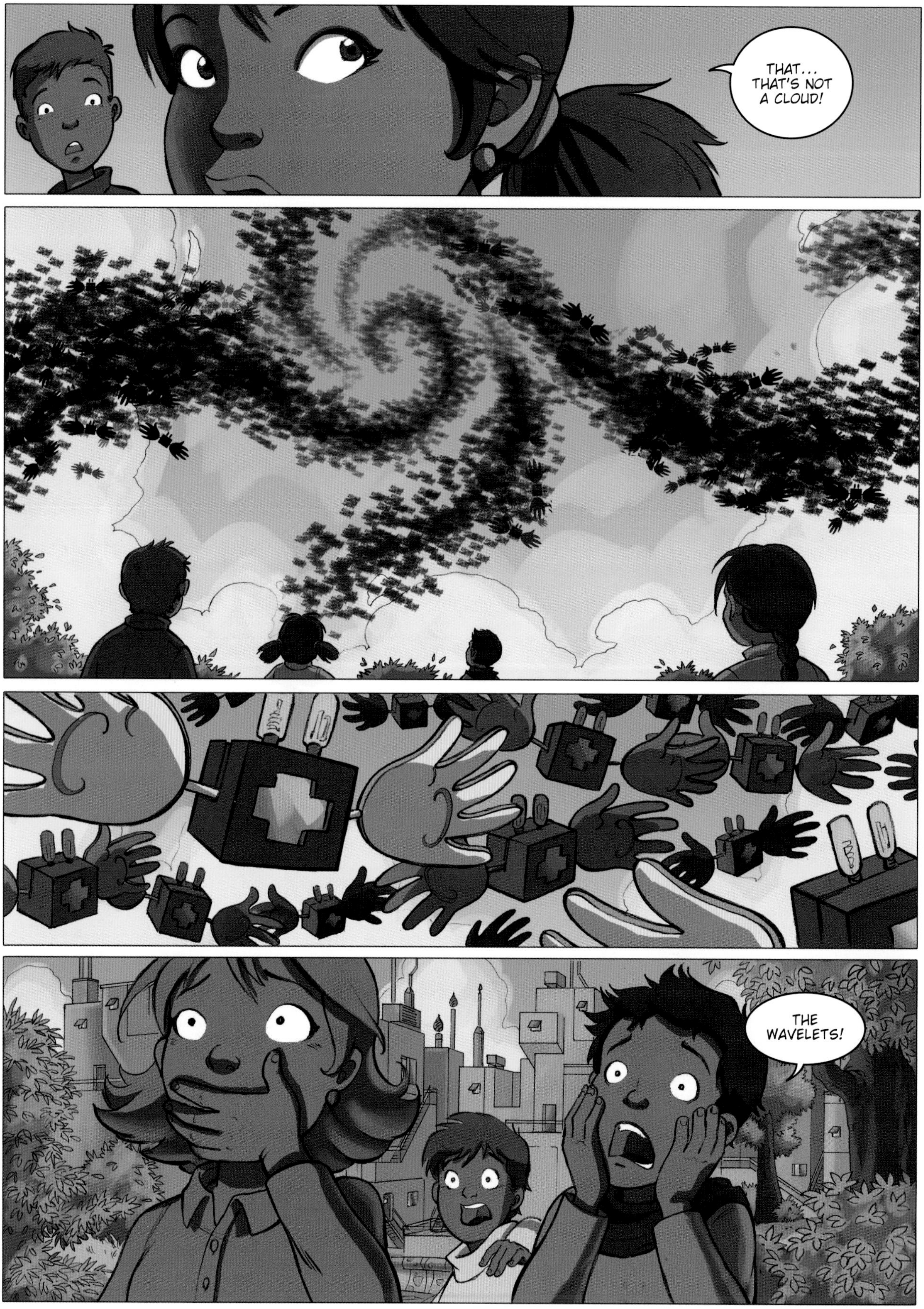
THAT... THAT'S NOT A CLOUD!
THE WAVELETS!

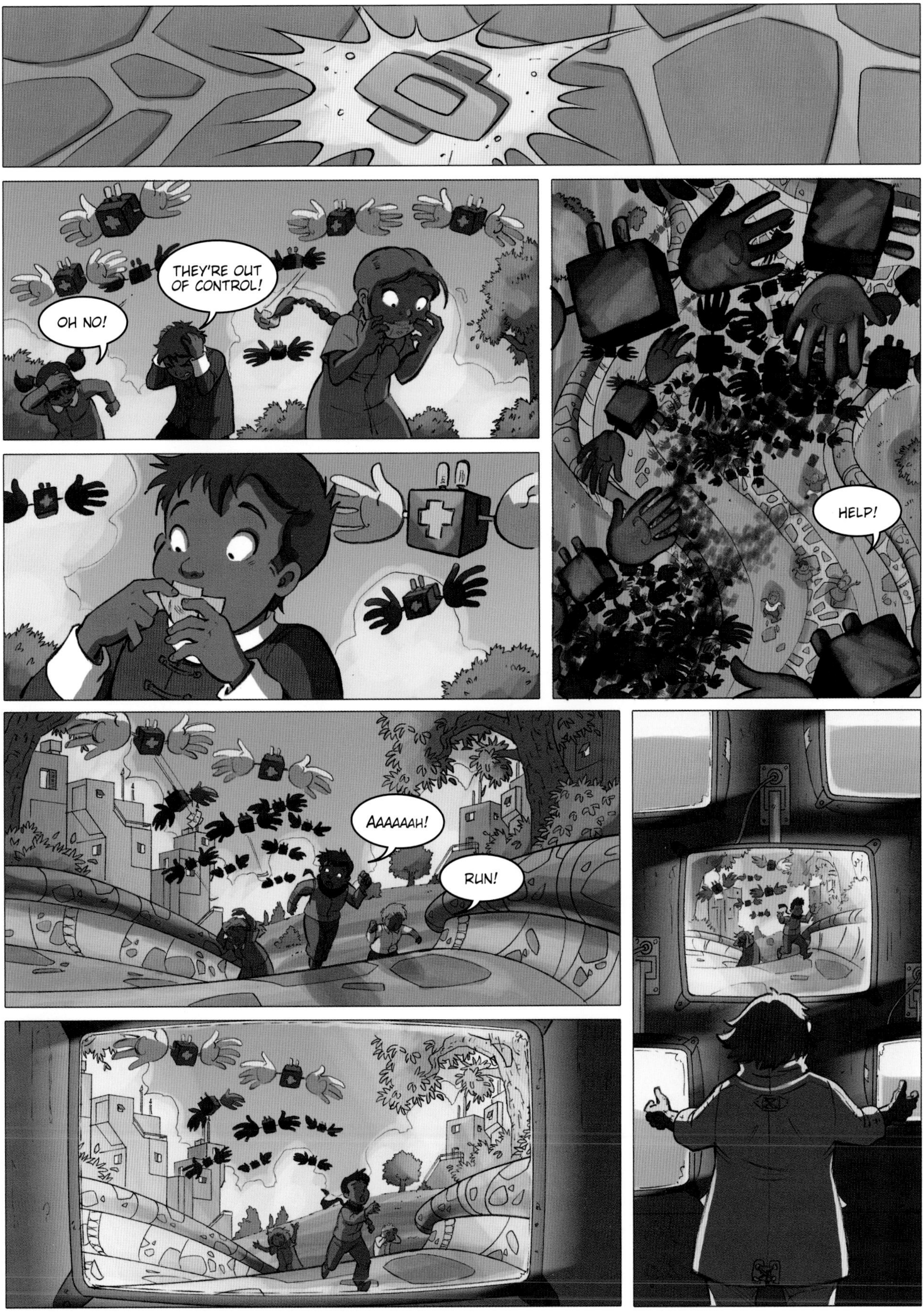
OH NO!
THEY'RE OUT OF CONTROL!
HELP!
AAAAAAH!
RUN!

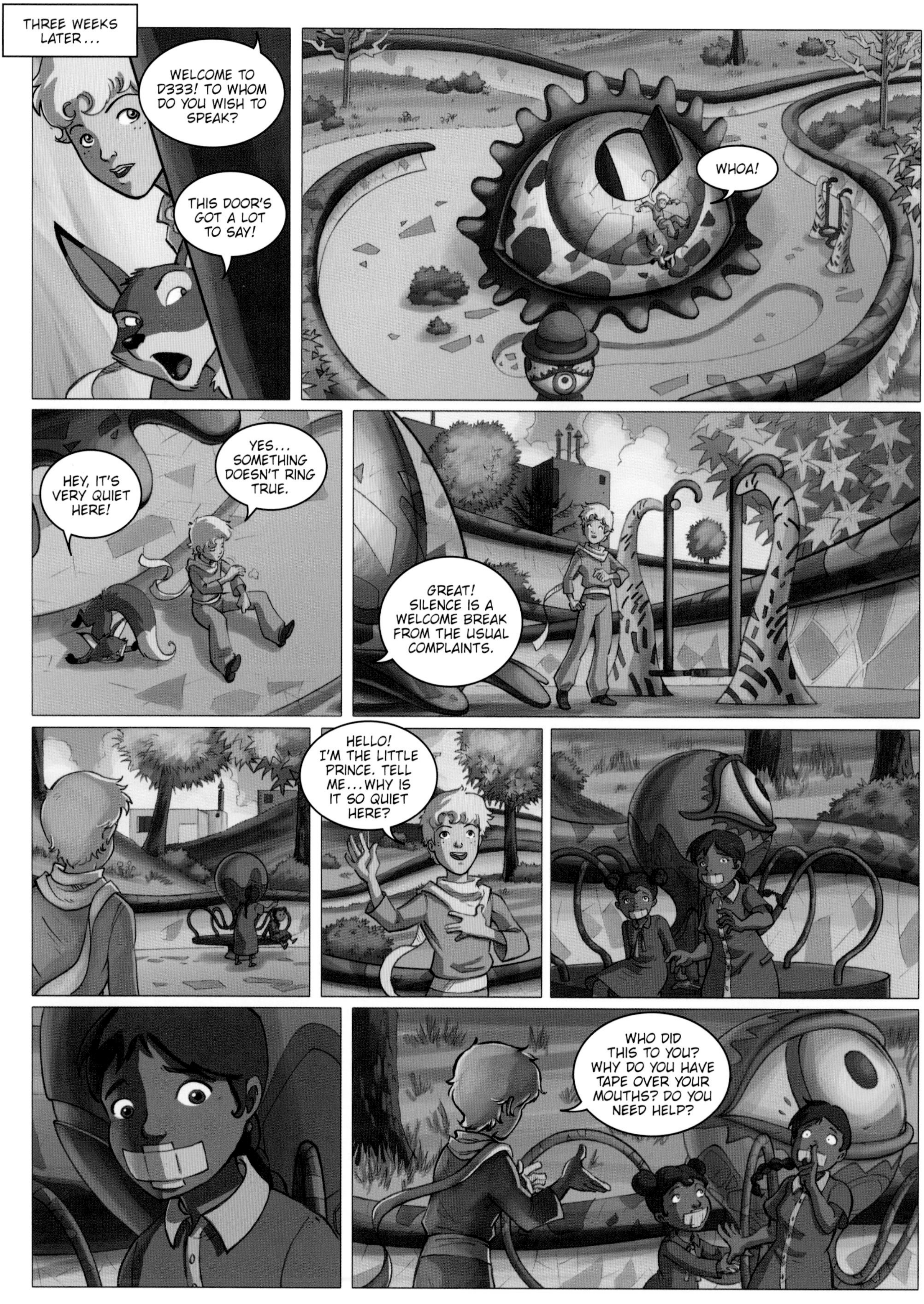
THREE WEEKS LATER...
WELCOME TO D333! TO WHOM DO YOU WISH TO SPEAK?
THIS DOOR'S GOT A LOT TO SAY!
WHOA!
HEY, IT'S VERY QUIET HERE!
YES... SOMETHING DOESN'T RING TRUE.
GREAT! SILENCE IS A WELCOME BREAK FROM THE USUAL COMPLAINTS.
HELLO! I'M THE LITTLE PRINCE. TELL ME...WHY IS IT SO QUIET HERE?
WHO DID THIS TO YOU? WHY DO YOU HAVE TAPE OVER YOUR MOUTHS? DO YOU NEED HELP?

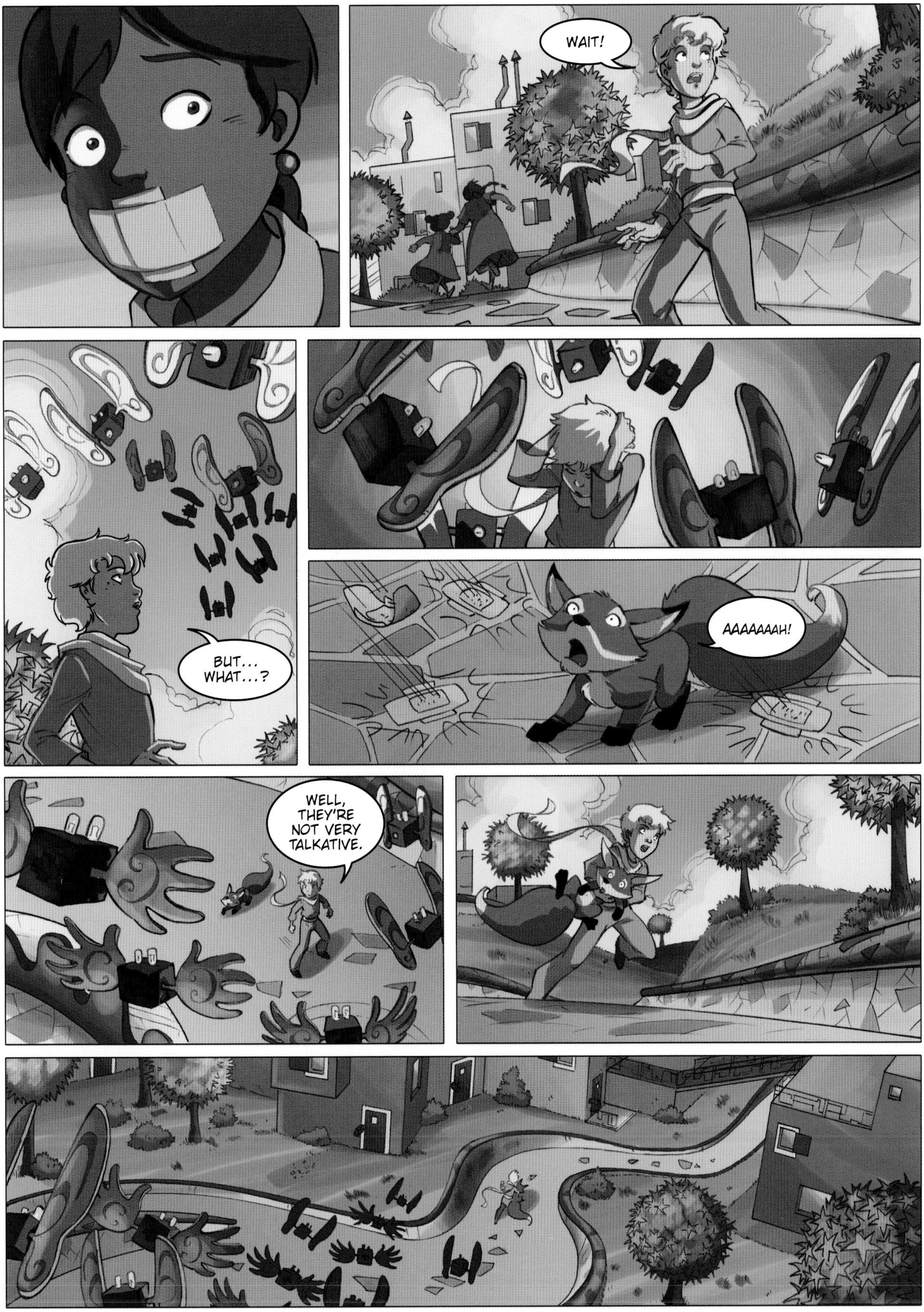
WAIT!
BUT... WHAT...?
AAAAAAAH!
WELL, THEY'RE NOT VERY TALKATIVE.

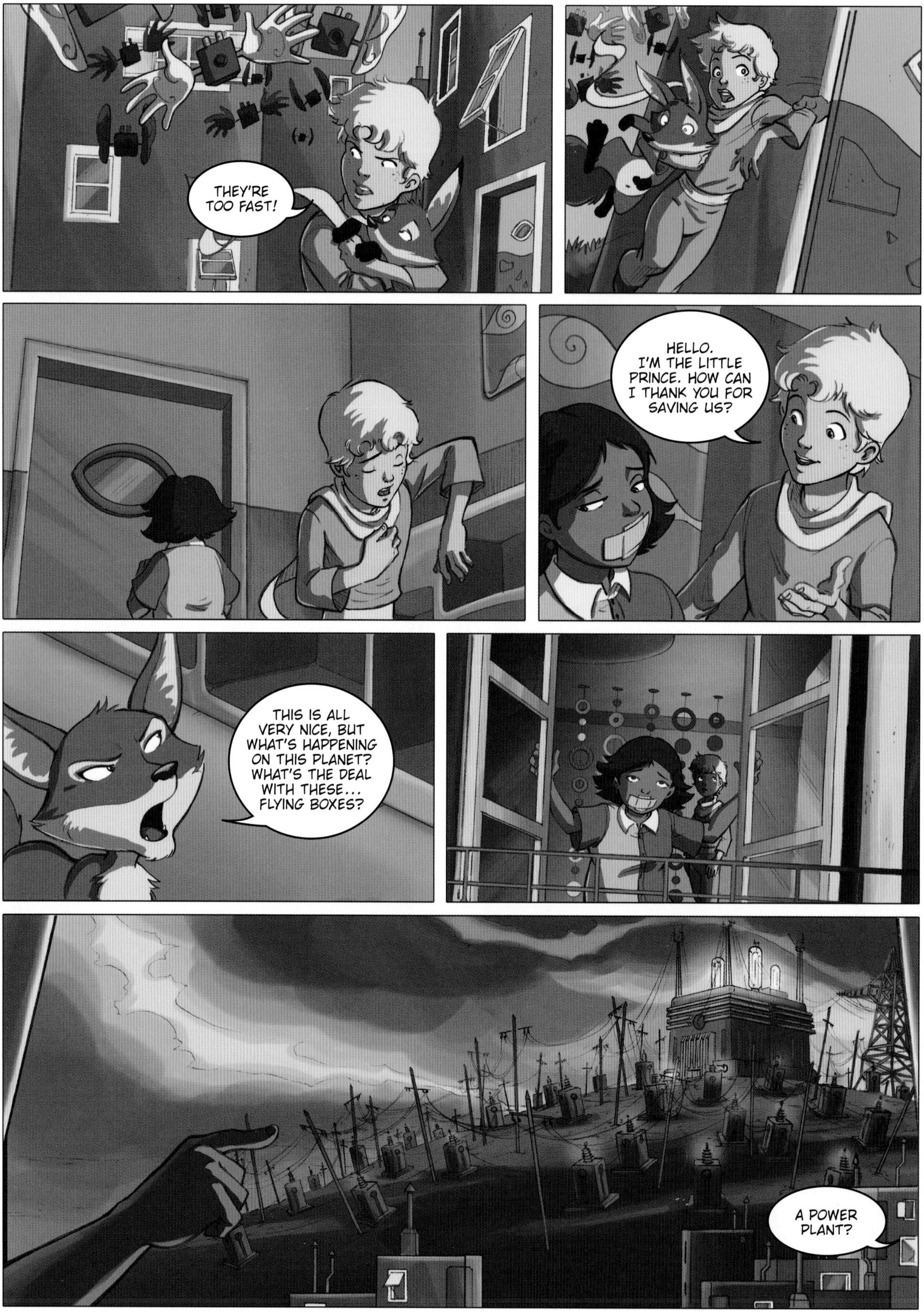
THEY'RE TOO FAST!
HELLO. I'M THE LITTLE PRINCE. HOW CAN I THANK YOU FOR SAVING US?
THIS IS ALL VERY NICE, BUT WHAT'S HAPPENING ON THIS PLANET? WHAT'S THE DEAL WITH THESE... FLYING BOXES?
A POWER PLANT?

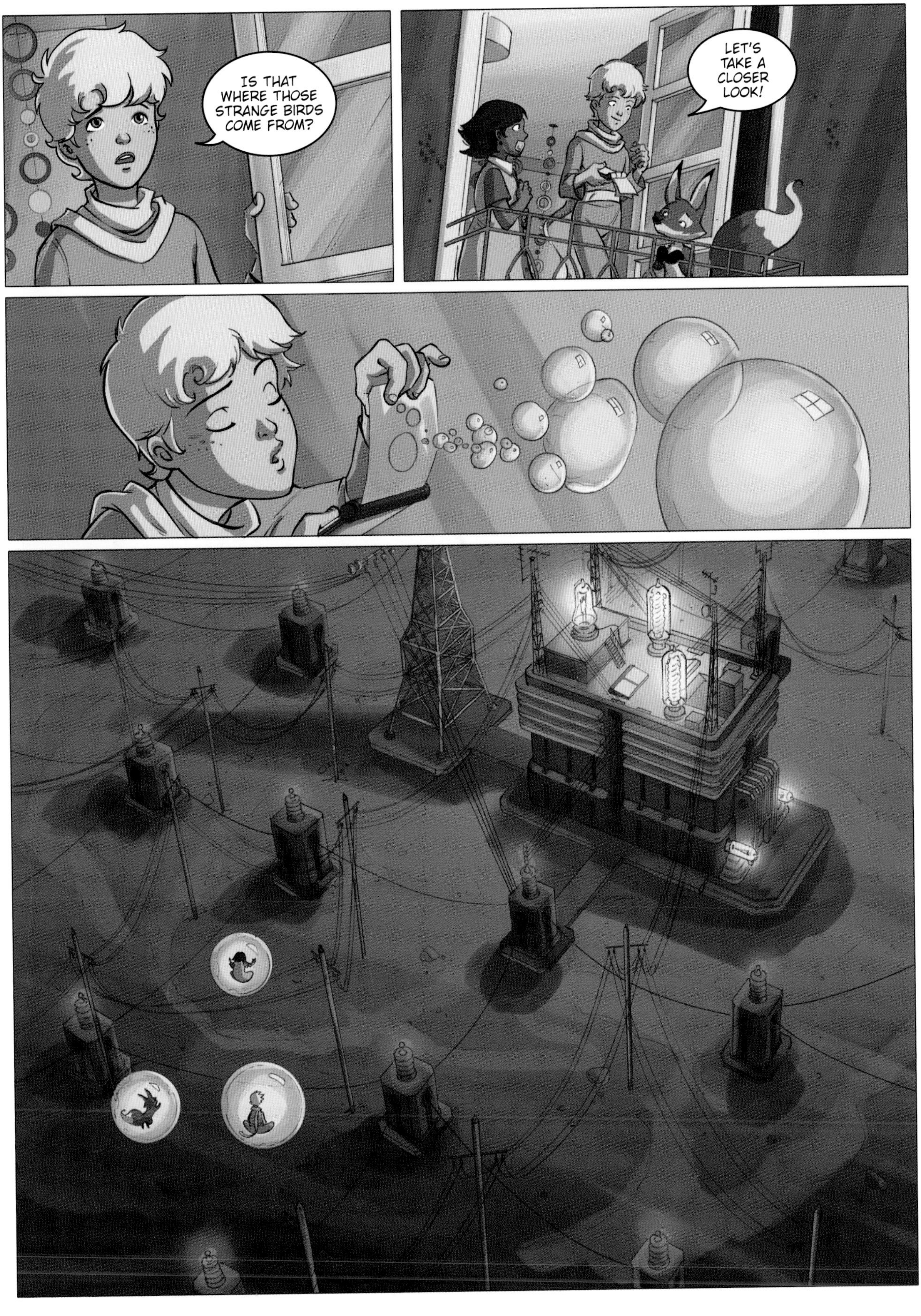
IS THAT WHERE THOSE STRANGE BIRDS COME FROM?
LET'S TAKE A CLOSER LOOK!

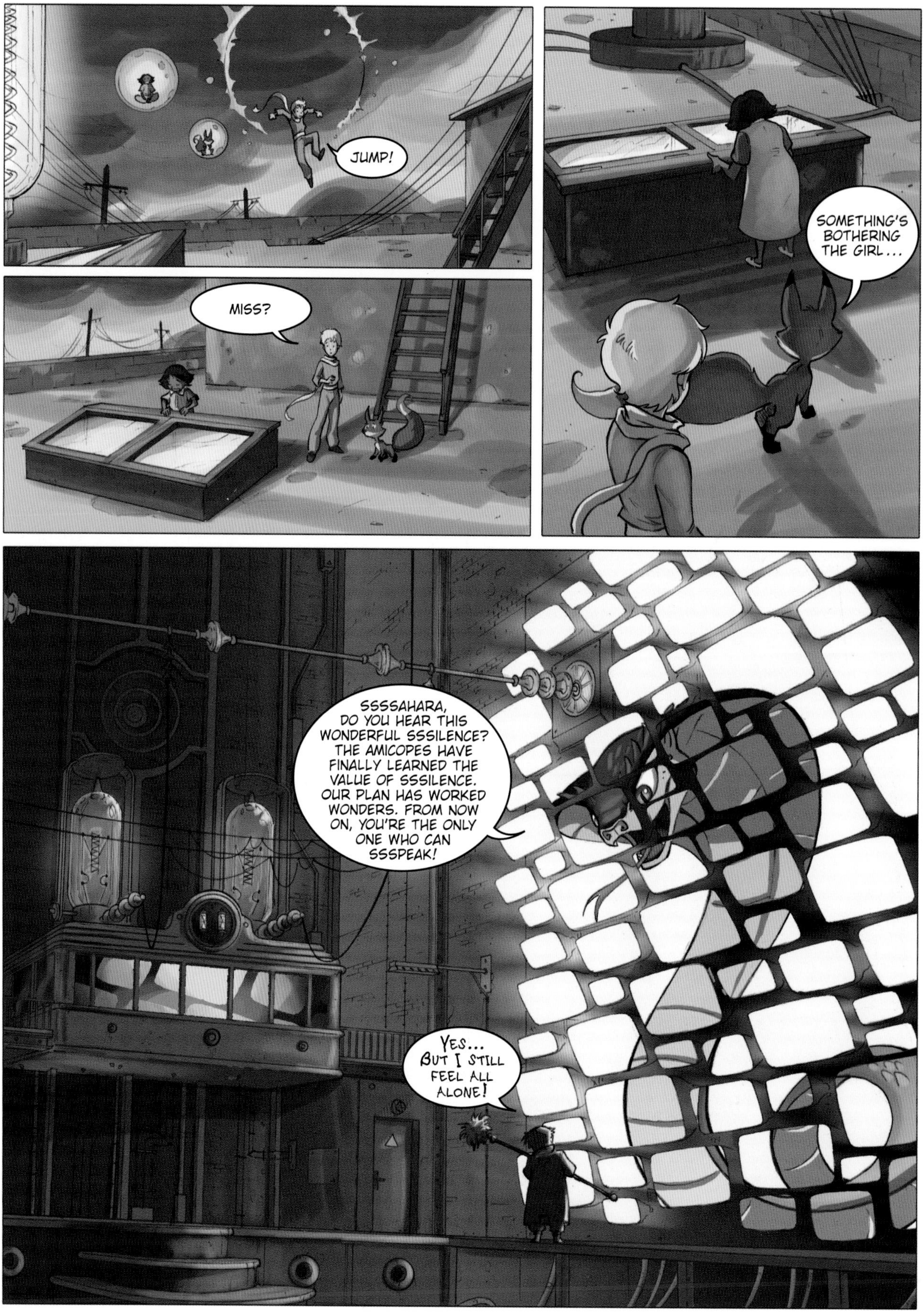
JUMP!
SOMETHING'S BOTHERING THE GIRL...
MISS?
SSSSAHARA, DO YOU HEAR THIS WONDERFUL SSSILENCE? THE AMICOPES HAVE FINALLY LEARNED THE VALUE OF SSSILENCE. OUR PLAN HAS WORKED WONDERS. FROM NOW ON, YOU'RE THE ONLY ONE WHO CAN SSSPEAK!
YES... BUT I STILL FEEL ALL ALONE!

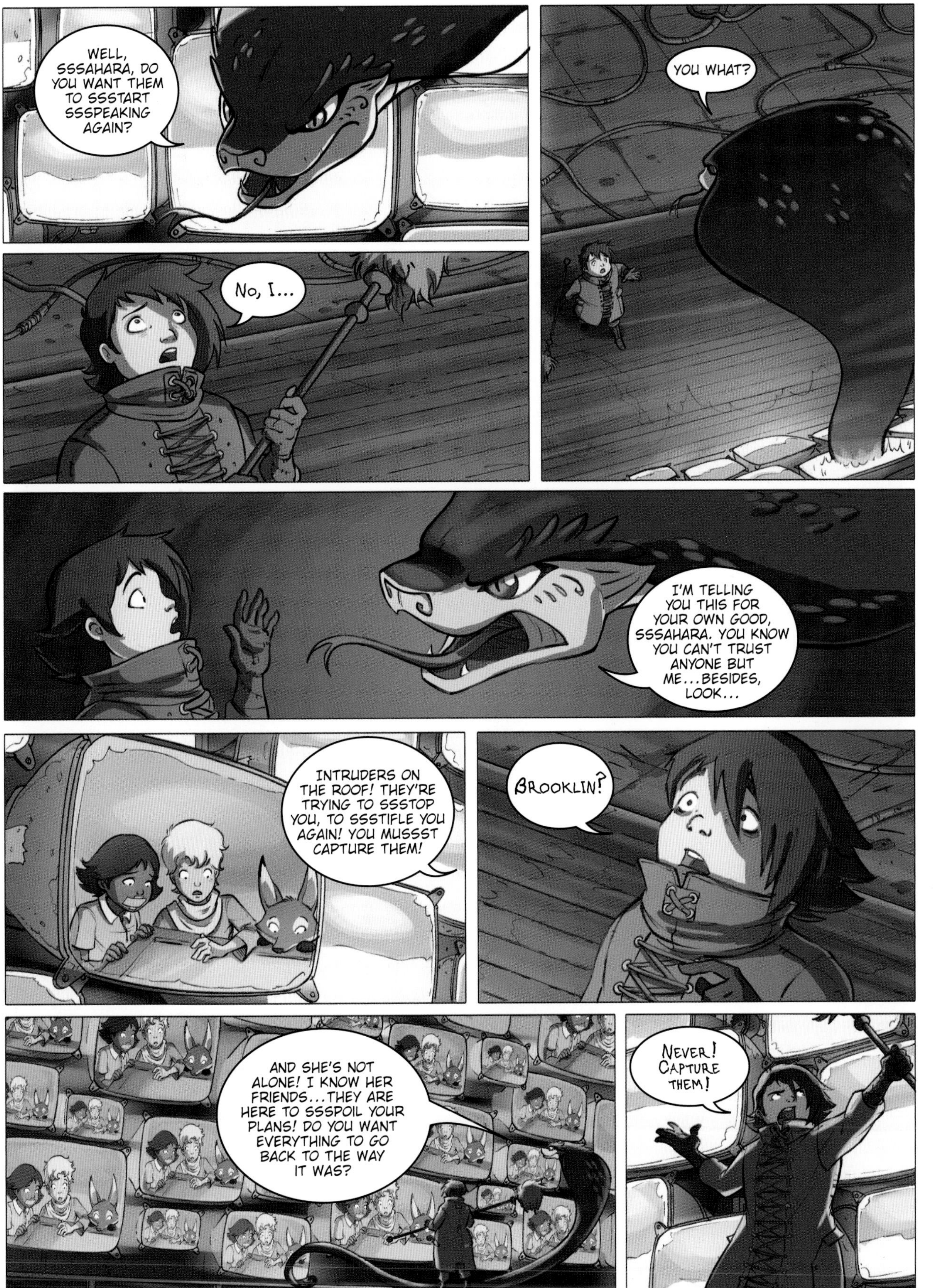
WELL, SSSAHARA, DO YOU WANT THEM TO SSSTART SSSPEAKING AGAIN?
YOU WHAT?
No, I...
I'M TELLING YOU THIS FOR YOUR OWN GOOD, SSSAHARA. YOU KNOW YOU CAN'T TRUST ANYONE BUT ME...BESIDES, LOOK...
INTRUDERS ON THE ROOF! THEY'RE TRYING TO SSSTOP YOU, TO SSSTIFLE YOU AGAIN! YOU MUSSST CAPTURE THEM!
BROOKLIN?
AND SHE'S NOT ALONE! I KNOW HER FRIENDS...THEY ARE HERE TO SSSPOIL YOUR PLANS! DO YOU WANT EVERYTHING TO GO BACK TO THE WAY IT WAS?
NEVER! CAPTURE THEM!

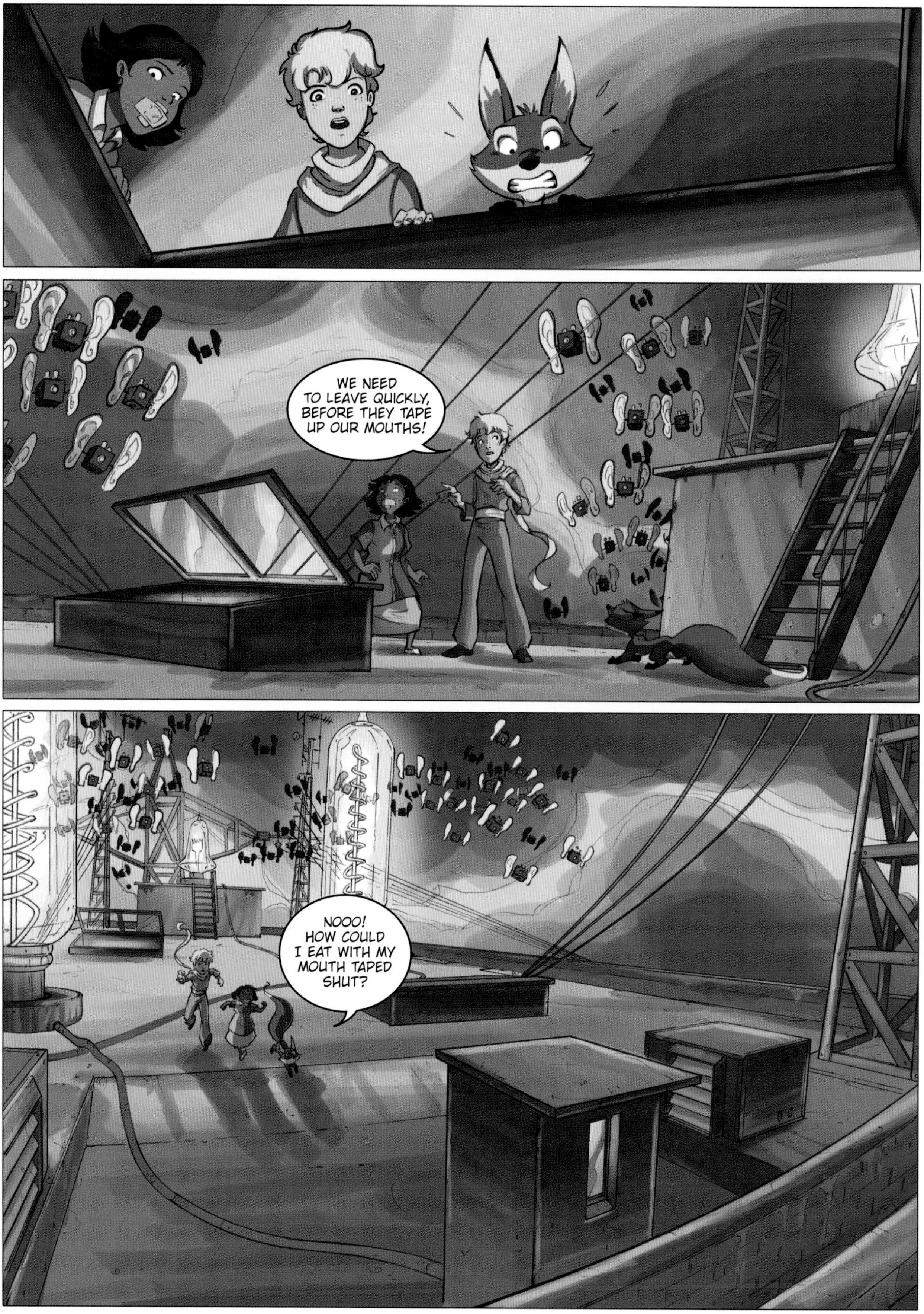
WE NEED TO LEAVE QUICKLY, BEFORE THEY TAPE UP OUR MOUTHS!
NOOO! HOW COULD I EAT WITH MY MOUTH TAPED SHUT?

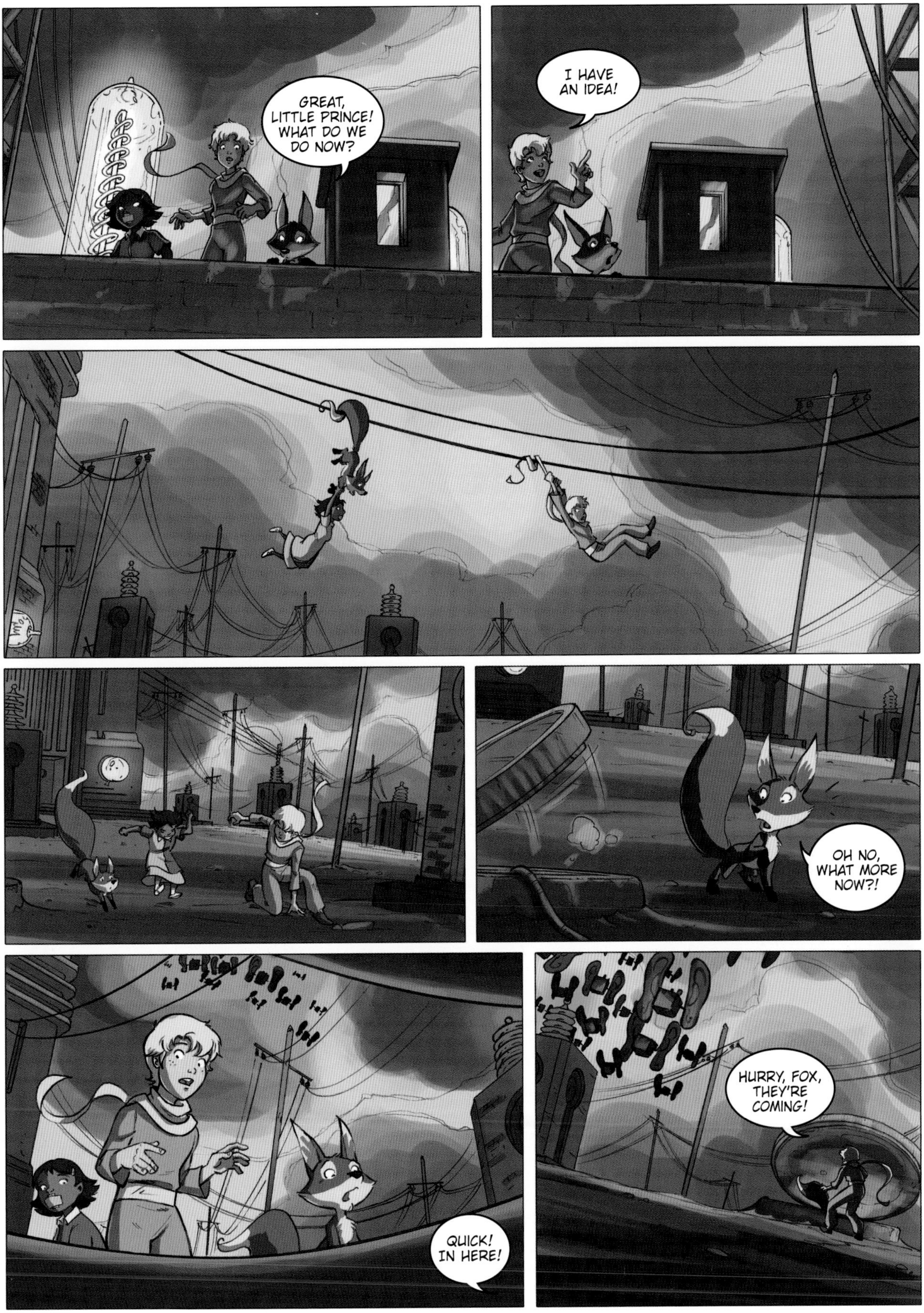
GREAT, LITTLE PRINCE! WHAT DO WE DO NOW?
I HAVE AN IDEA!
OH NO, WHAT MORE NOW?!
QUICK! IN HERE!
HURRY, FOX, THEY'RE COMING!

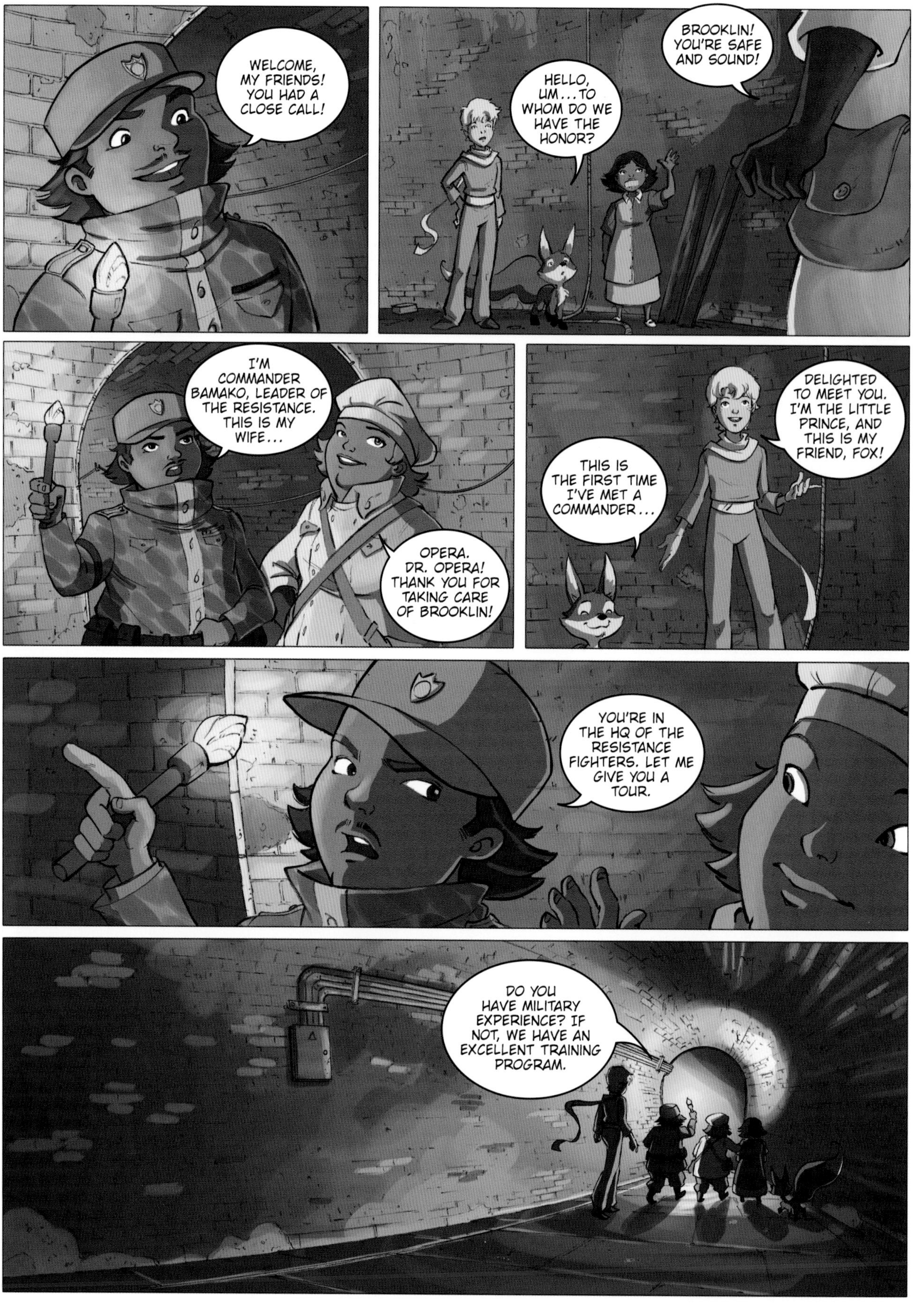
WELCOME, MY FRIENDS! YOU HAD A CLOSE CALL!
HELLO, UM...TO WHOM DO WE HAVE THE HONOR?
BROOKLIN! YOU'RE SAFE AND SOUND!
I'M COMMANDER BAMAKO, LEADER OF THE RESISTANCE. THIS IS MY WIFE...
OPERA. DR. OPERA! THANK YOU FOR TAKING CARE OF BROOKLIN!
DELIGHTED TO MEET YOU. I'M THE LITTLE PRINCE, AND THIS IS MY FRIEND, FOX!
THIS IS THE FIRST TIME I'VE MET A COMMANDER...
YOU'RE IN THE HQ OF THE RESISTANCE FIGHTERS. LET ME GIVE YOU A TOUR.
DO YOU HAVE MILITARY EXPERIENCE? IF NOT, WE HAVE AN EXCELLENT TRAINING PROGRAM.

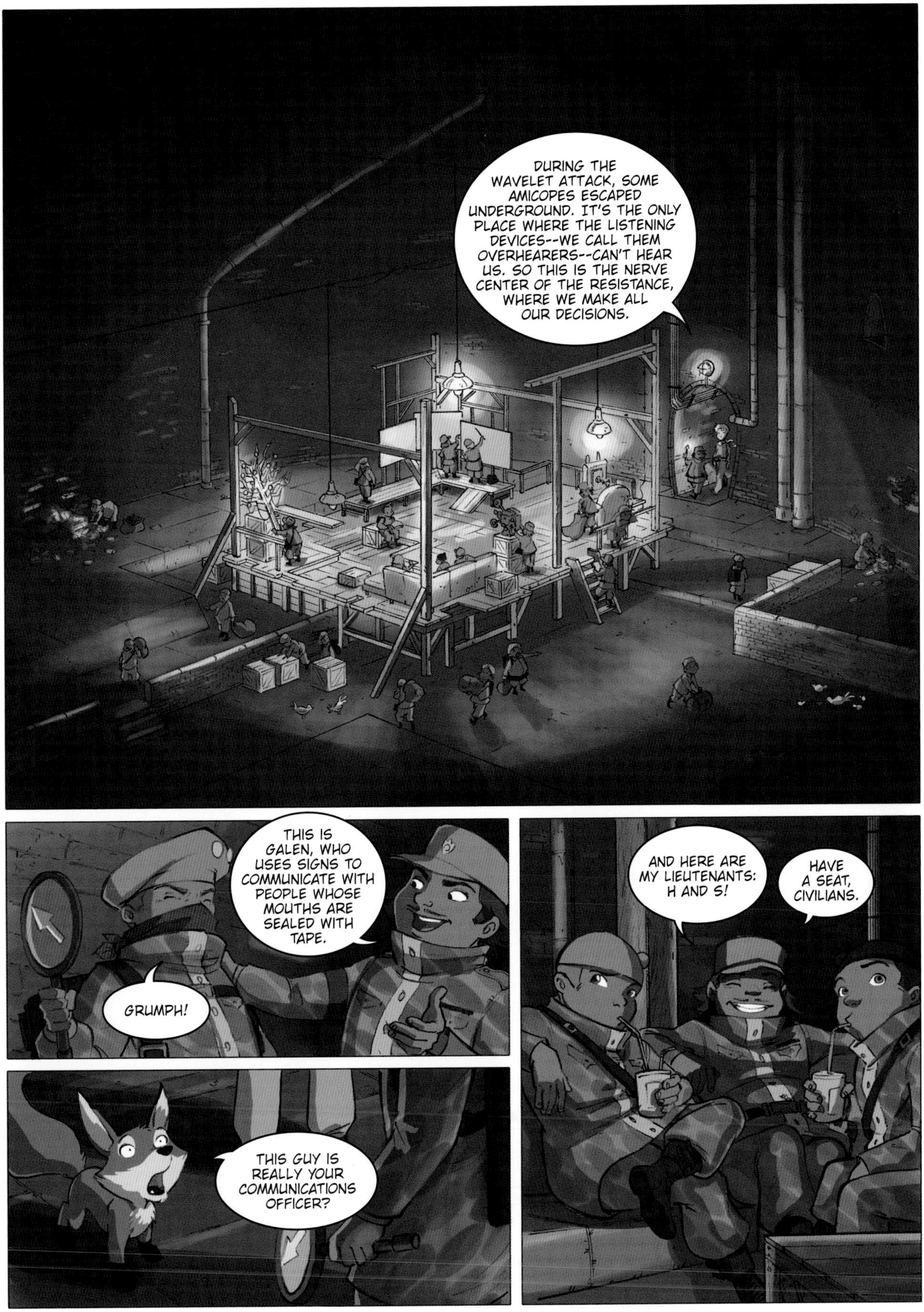
DURING THE WAVELET ATTACK, SOME AMICOPES ESCAPED UNDERGROUND. IT'S THE ONLY PLACE WHERE THE LISTENING DEVICES--WE CALL THEM OVERHEARERS--CAN'T HEAR US. SO THIS IS THE NERVE CENTER OF THE RESISTANCE, WHERE WE MAKE ALL OUR DECISIONS.
THIS IS GALEN, WHO USES SIGNS TO COMMUNICATE WITH PEOPLE WHOSE MOUTHS ARE SEALED WITH TAPE.
GRUMPH!
THIS GUY IS REALLY YOUR COMMUNICATIONS OFFICER?
AND HERE ARE MY LIEUTENANTS: H AND S!
HAVE A SEAT, CIVILIANS.

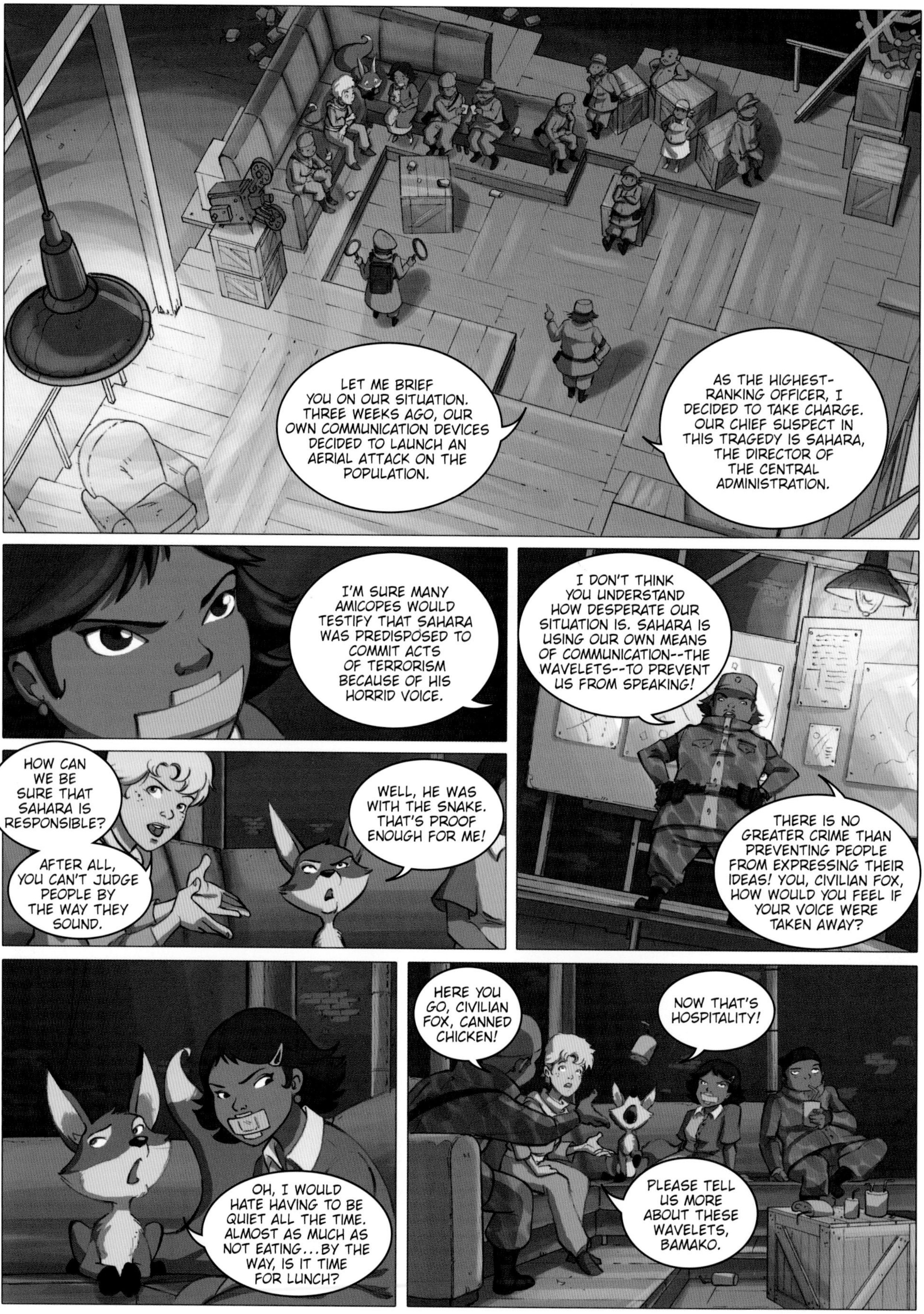
LET ME BRIEF YOU ON OUR SITUATION. THREE WEEKS AGO, OUR OWN COMMUNICATION DEVICES DECIDED TO LAUNCH AN AERIAL ATTACK ON THE POPULATION.
AS THE HIGHEST-RANKING OFFICER, I DECIDED TO TAKE CHARGE. OUR CHIEF SUSPECT IN THIS TRAGEDY IS SAHARA, THE DIRECTOR OF THE CENTRAL ADMINISTRATION.
I'M SURE MANY AMICOPES WOULD TESTIFY THAT SAHARA WAS PREDISPOSED TO COMMIT ACTS OF TERRORISM BECAUSE OF HIS HORRID VOICE.
I DON'T THINK YOU UNDERSTAND HOW DESPERATE OUR SITUATION IS. SAHARA IS USING OUR OWN MEANS OF COMMUNICATION--THE WAVELETS--TO PREVENT US FROM SPEAKING!
HOW CAN WE BE SURE THAT SAHARA IS RESPONSIBLE?
AFTER ALL, YOU CAN'T JUDGE PEOPLE BY THE WAY THEY SOUND.
WELL, HE WAS WITH THE SNAKE. THAT'S PROOF ENOUGH FOR ME!
THERE IS NO GREATER CRIME THAN PREVENTING PEOPLE FROM EXPRESSING THEIR IDEAS! YOU, CIVILIAN FOX, HOW WOULD YOU FEEL IF YOUR VOICE WERE TAKEN AWAY?
OH, I WOULD HATE HAVING TO BE QUIET ALL THE TIME. ALMOST AS MUCH AS NOT EATING... BY THE WAY, IS IT TIME FOR LUNCH?
HERE YOU GO, CIVILIAN FOX, CANNED CHICKEN!
NOW THAT'S HOSPITALITY!
PLEASE TELL US MORE ABOUT THESE WAVELETS, BAMAKO.

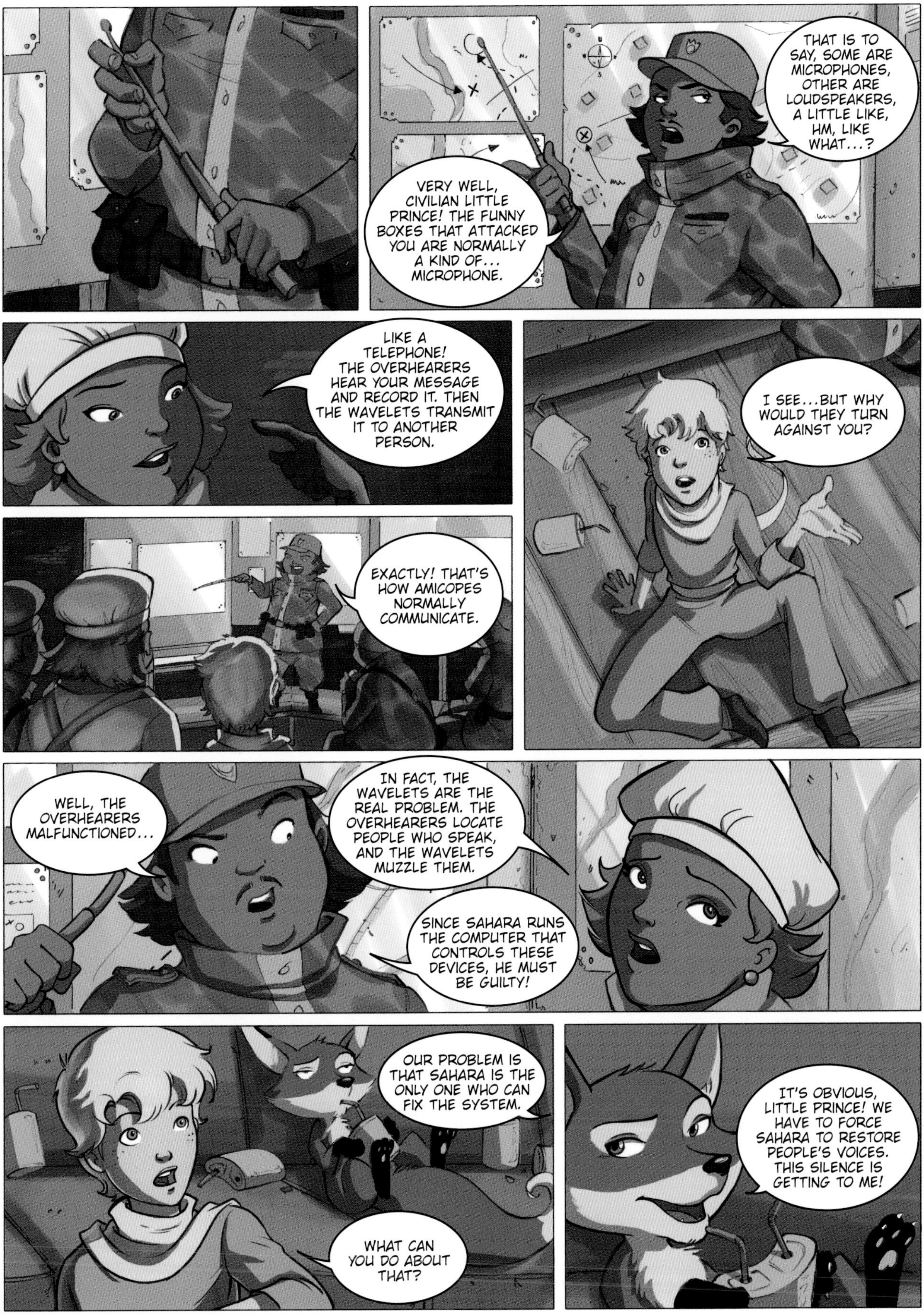
VERY WELL, CIVILIAN LITTLE PRINCE! THE FUNNY BOXES THAT ATTACKED YOU ARE NORMALLY A KIND OF... MICROPHONE.
THAT IS TO SAY, SOME ARE MICROPHONES, OTHER ARE LOUDSPEAKERS, A LITTLE LIKE, HM, LIKE WHAT...?
LIKE A TELEPHONE! THE OVERHEARERS HEAR YOUR MESSAGE AND RECORD IT. THEN THE WAVELETS TRANSMIT IT TO ANOTHER PERSON.
EXACTLY! THAT'S HOW AMICOPES NORMALLY COMMUNICATE.
I SEE...BUT WHY WOULD THEY TURN AGAINST YOU?
WELL, THE OVERHEARERS MALFUNCTIONED...
IN FACT, THE WAVELETS ARE THE REAL PROBLEM. THE OVERHEARERS LOCATE PEOPLE WHO SPEAK, AND THE WAVELETS MUZZLE THEM.
SINCE SAHARA RUNS THE COMPUTER THAT CONTROLS THESE DEVICES, HE MUST BE GUILTY!
OUR PROBLEM IS THAT SAHARA IS THE ONLY ONE WHO CAN FIX THE SYSTEM.
WHAT CAN YOU DO ABOUT THAT?
IT'S OBVIOUS, LITTLE PRINCE! WE HAVE TO FORCE SAHARA TO RESTORE PEOPLE'S VOICES. THIS SILENCE IS GETTING TO ME!

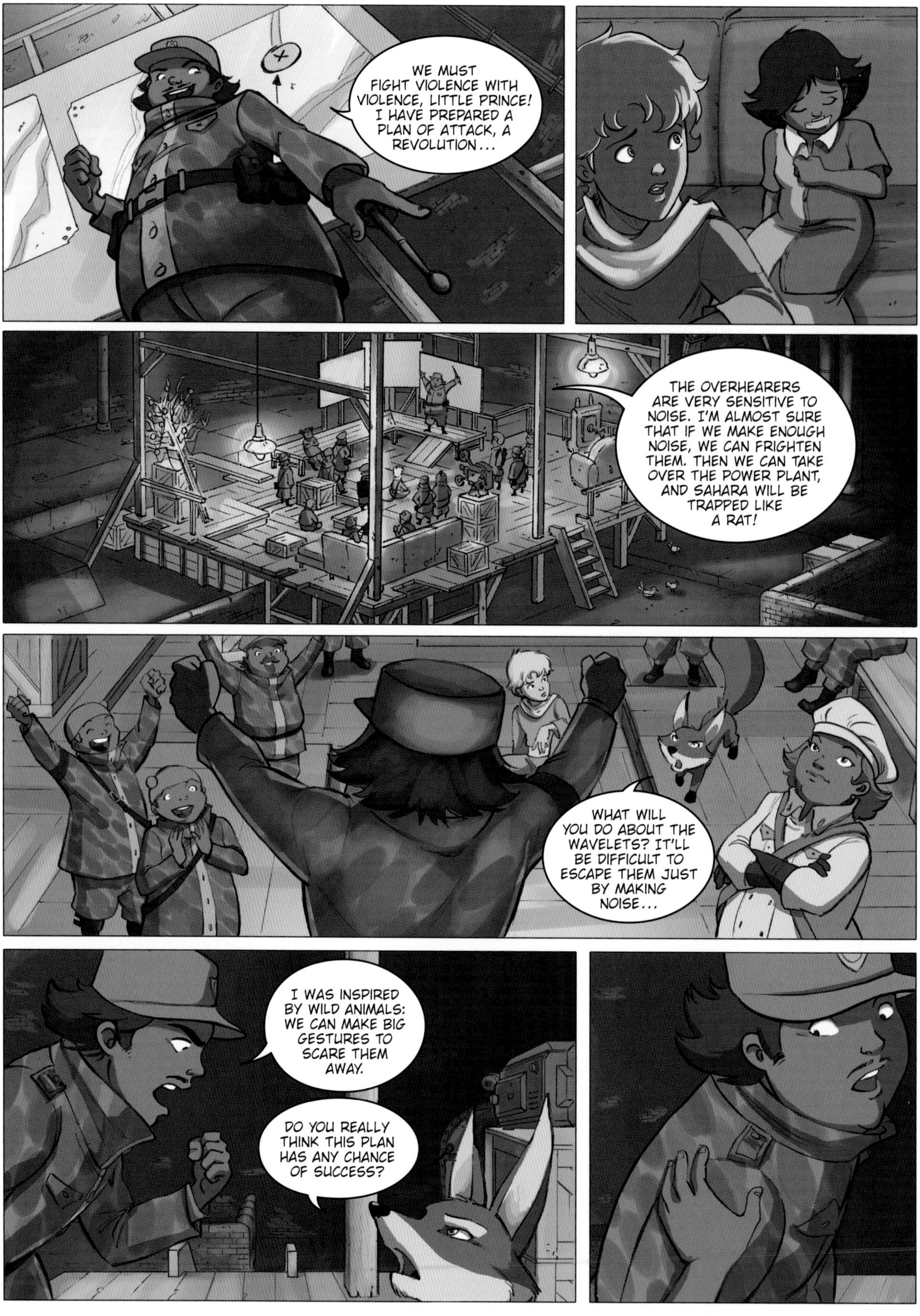
WE MUST FIGHT VIOLENCE WITH VIOLENCE, LITTLE PRINCE! I HAVE PREPARED A PLAN OF ATTACK, A REVOLUTION...
THE OVERHEARERS ARE VERY SENSITIVE TO NOISE. I'M ALMOST SURE THAT IF WE MAKE ENOUGH NOISE, WE CAN FRIGHTEN THEM. THEN WE CAN TAKE OVER THE POWER PLANT, AND SAHARA WILL BE TRAPPED LIKE A RAT!
WHAT WILL YOU DO ABOUT THE WAVELETS? IT'LL BE DIFFICULT TO ESCAPE THEM JUST BY MAKING NOISE...
I WAS INSPIRED BY WILD ANIMALS: WE CAN MAKE BIG GESTURES TO SCARE THEM AWAY.
DO YOU REALLY THINK THIS PLAN HAS ANY CHANCE OF SUCCESS?

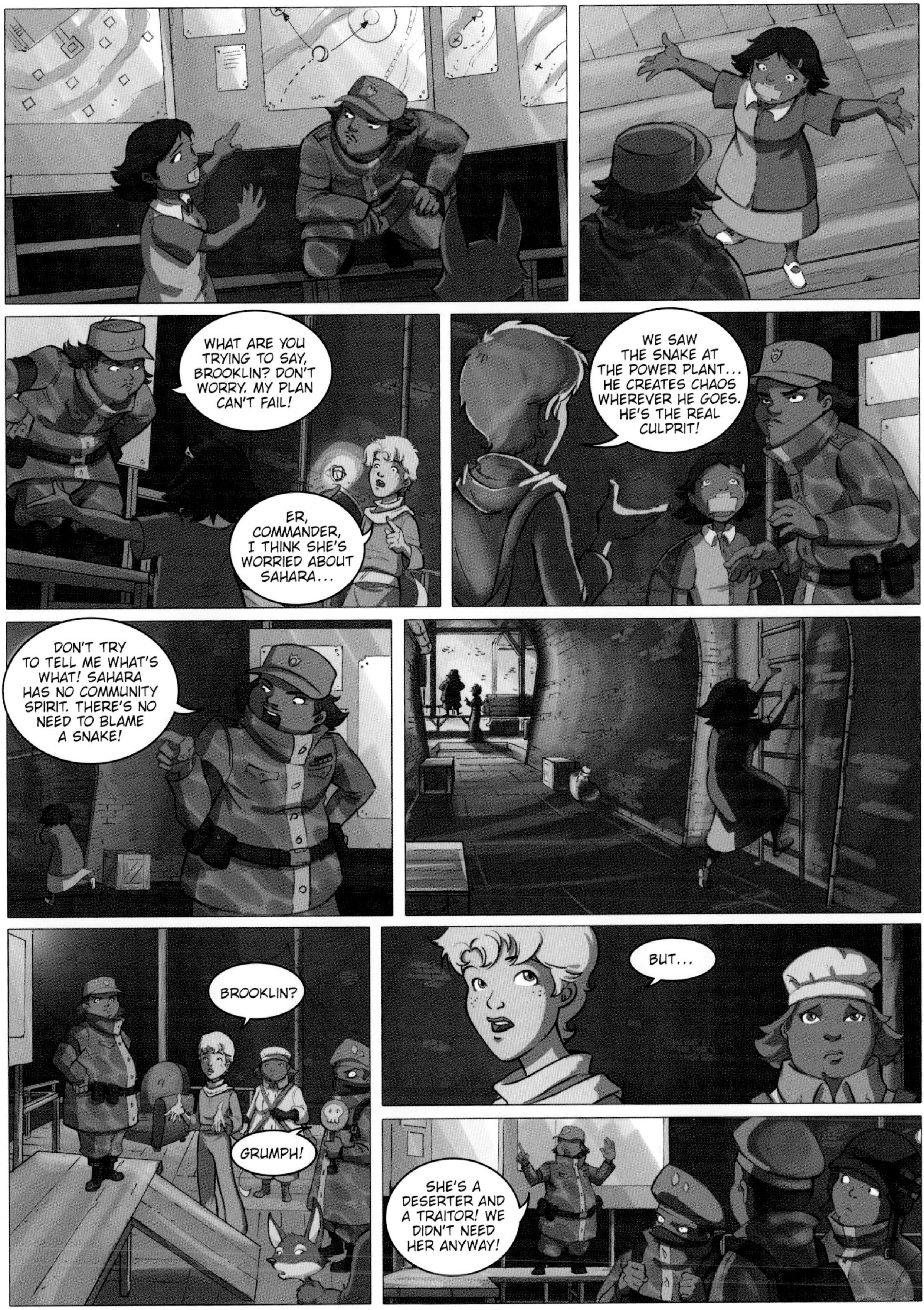

WHAT ARE YOU TRYING TO SAY, BROOKLIN? DON'T WORRY. MY PLAN CAN'T FAIL!
ER, COMMANDER, I THINK SHE'S WORRIED ABOUT SAHARA...
WE SAW THE SNAKE AT THE POWER PLANT... HE CREATES CHAOS WHEREVER HE GOES. HE'S THE REAL CULPRIT!
DON'T TRY TO TELL ME WHAT'S WHAT! SAHARA HAS NO COMMUNITY SPIRIT. THERE'S NO NEED TO BLAME A SNAKE!
BROOKLIN?
GRUMPH!
BUT...
SHE'S A DESERTER AND A TRAITOR! WE DIDN'T NEED HER ANYWAY!

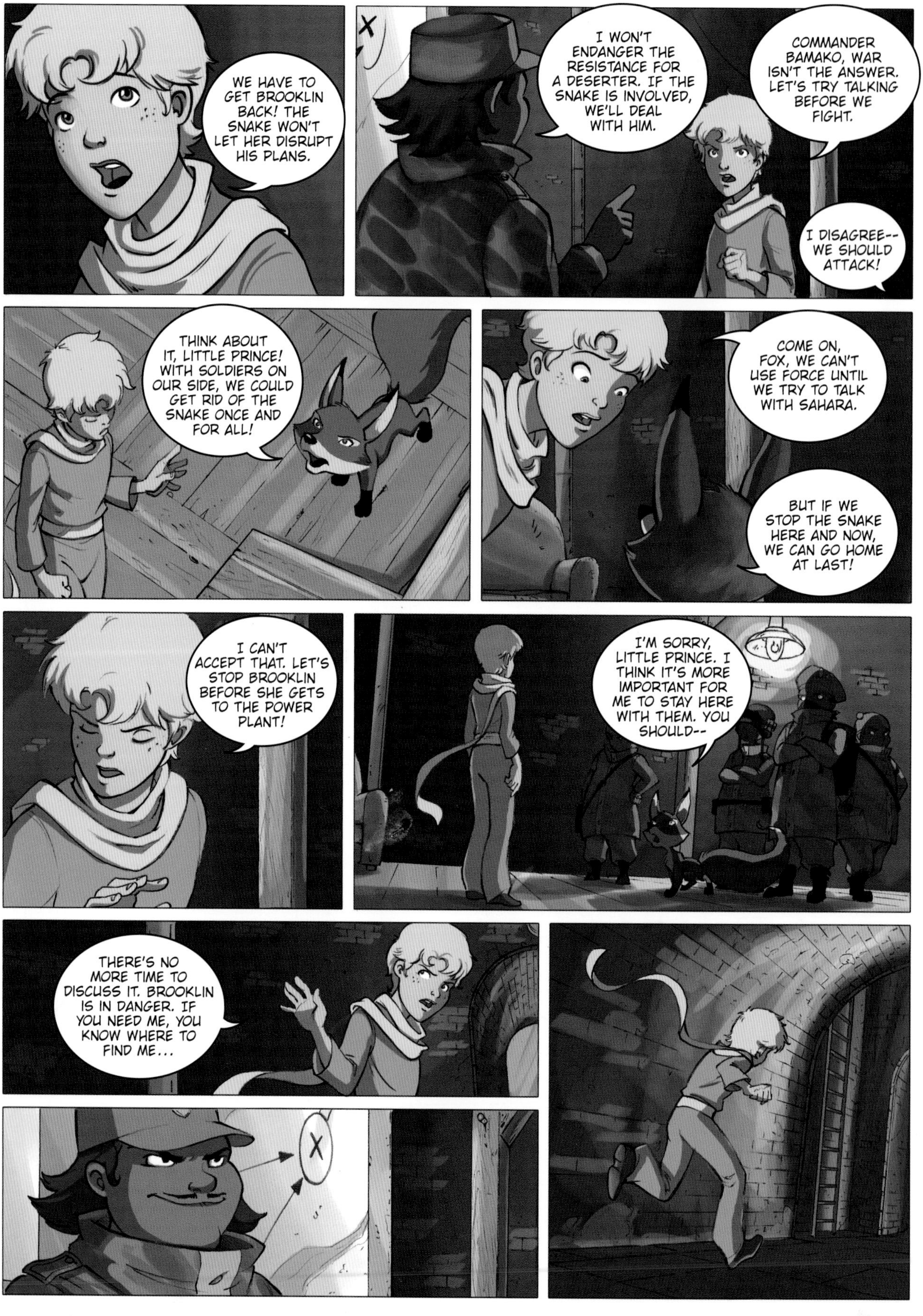
WE HAVE TO GET BROOKLIN BACK! THE SNAKE WON'T LET HER DISRUPT HIS PLANS.
I WON'T ENDANGER THE RESISTANCE FOR A DESERTER. IF THE SNAKE IS INVOLVED, WE'LL DEAL WITH HIM.
COMMANDER BAMAKO, WAR ISN'T THE ANSWER. LET'S TRY TALKING BEFORE WE FIGHT.
I DISAGREE--WE SHOULD ATTACK!
THINK ABOUT IT, LITTLE PRINCE! WITH SOLDIERS ON OUR SIDE, WE COULD GET RID OF THE SNAKE ONCE AND FOR ALL!
COME ON, FOX, WE CAN'T USE FORCE UNTIL WE TRY TO TALK WITH SAHARA.
BUT IF WE STOP THE SNAKE HERE AND NOW, WE CAN GO HOME AT LAST!
I CAN'T ACCEPT THAT. LET'S STOP BROOKLIN BEFORE SHE GETS TO THE POWER PLANT!
I'M SORRY, LITTLE PRINCE. I THINK IT'S MORE IMPORTANT FOR ME TO STAY HERE WITH THEM. YOU SHOULD--
THERE'S NO MORE TIME TO DISCUSS IT. BROOKLIN IS IN DANGER. IF YOU NEED ME, YOU KNOW WHERE TO FIND ME...

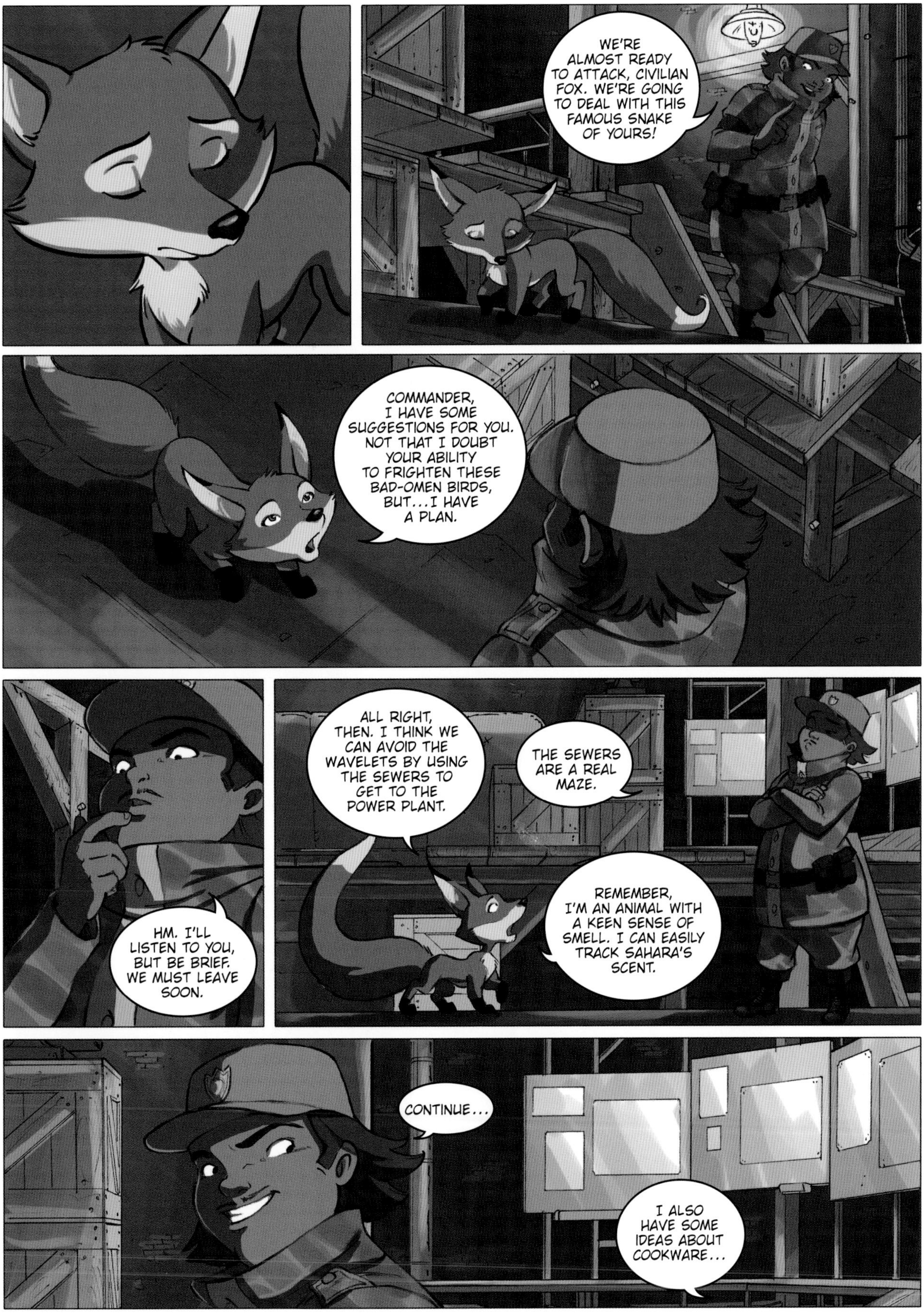
WE'RE ALMOST READY TO ATTACK, CIVILIAN FOX. WE'RE GOING TO DEAL WITH THIS FAMOUS SNAKE OF YOURS!
COMMANDER, I HAVE SOME SUGGESTIONS FOR YOU. NOT THAT I DOUBT YOUR ABILITY TO FRIGHTEN THESE BAD-OMEN BIRDS, BUT... I HAVE A PLAN.
HM. I'LL LISTEN TO YOU, BUT BE BRIEF. WE MUST LEAVE SOON.
ALL RIGHT, THEN. I THINK WE CAN AVOID THE WAVELETS BY USING THE SEWERS TO GET TO THE POWER PLANT.
THE SEWERS ARE A REAL MAZE.
REMEMBER, I'M AN ANIMAL WITH A KEEN SENSE OF SMELL. I CAN EASILY TRACK SAHARA'S SCENT.
CONTINUE...
I ALSO HAVE SOME IDEAS ABOUT COOKWARE...

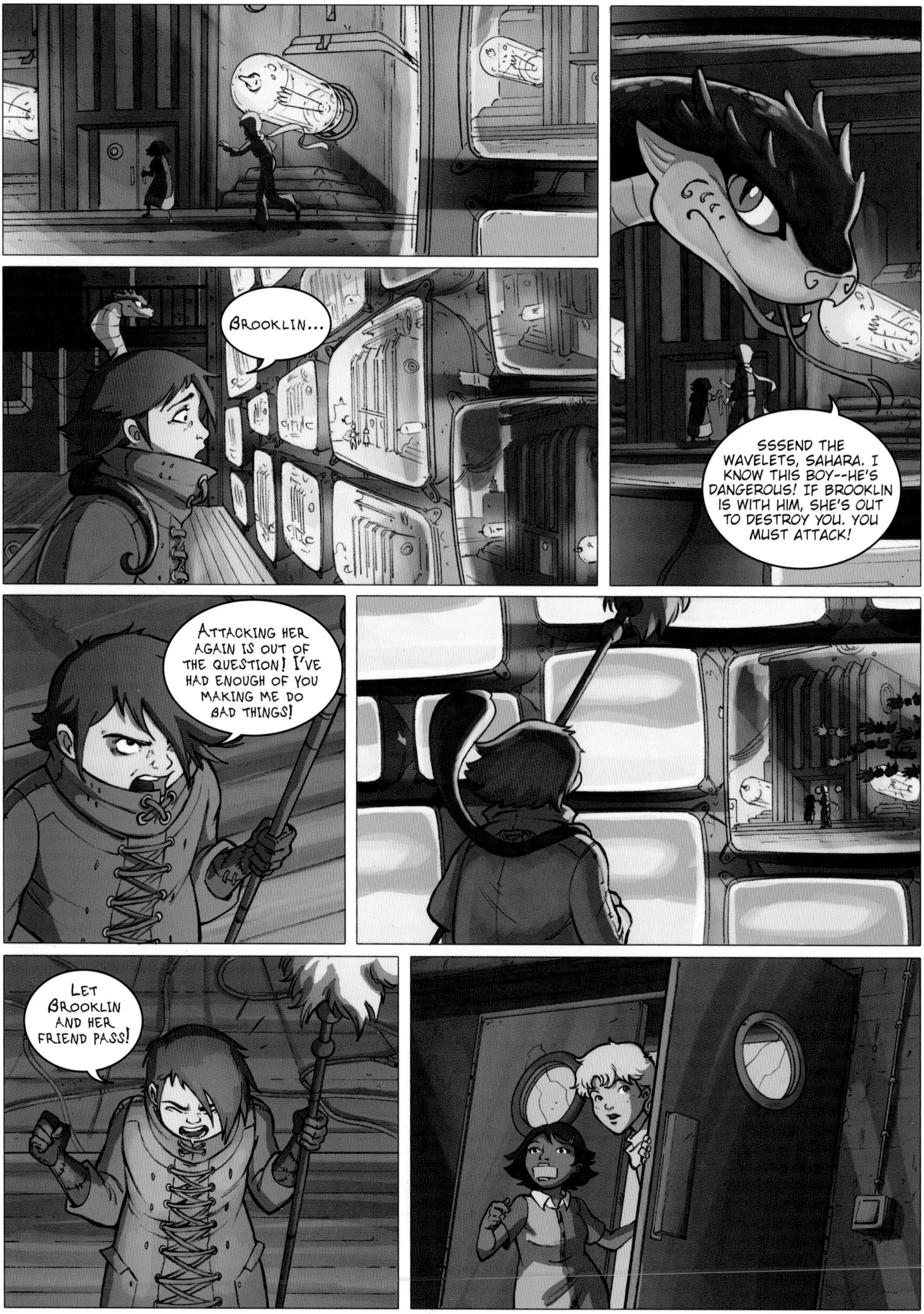
Brooklin...
Sssend the wavelets, Sahara. I know this boy--he's dangerous! If Brooklin is with him, she's out to destroy you. You must attack!
Attacking her again is out of the question! I've had enough of you making me do bad things!
Let Brooklin and her friend pass!

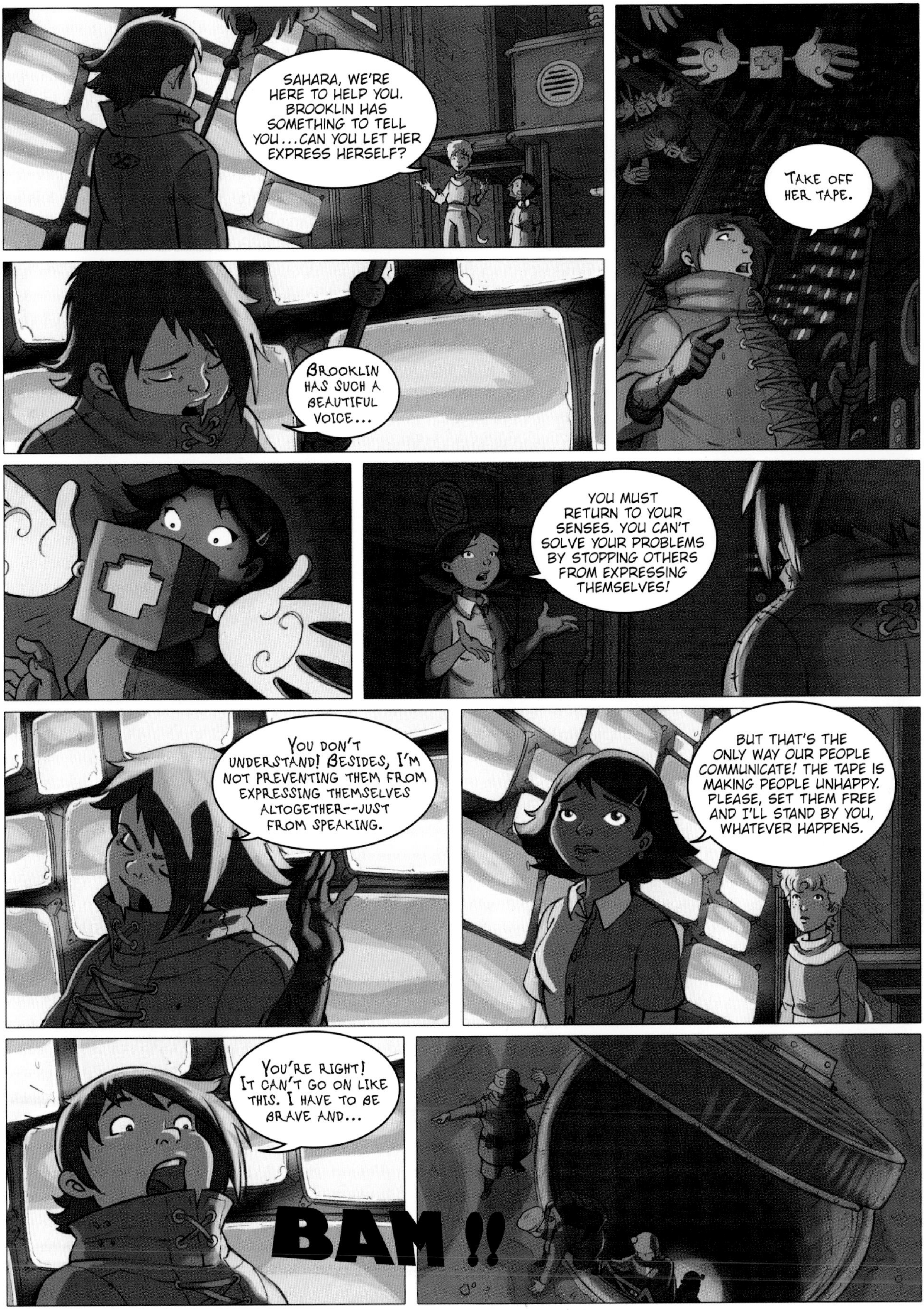
SAHARA, WE'RE HERE TO HELP YOU. BROOKLIN HAS SOMETHING TO TELL YOU...CAN YOU LET HER EXPRESS HERSELF?
TAKE OFF HER TAPE.
BROOKLIN HAS SUCH A BEAUTIFUL VOICE...
YOU MUST RETURN TO YOUR SENSES. YOU CAN'T SOLVE YOUR PROBLEMS BY STOPPING OTHERS FROM EXPRESSING THEMSELVES!
YOU DON'T UNDERSTAND! BESIDES, I'M NOT PREVENTING THEM FROM EXPRESSING THEMSELVES ALTOGETHER--JUST FROM SPEAKING.
BUT THAT'S THE ONLY WAY OUR PEOPLE COMMUNICATE! THE TAPE IS MAKING PEOPLE UNHAPPY. PLEASE, SET THEM FREE AND I'LL STAND BY YOU, WHATEVER HAPPENS.
YOU'RE RIGHT! IT CAN'T GO ON LIKE THIS. I HAVE TO BE BRAVE AND...
BAM !!

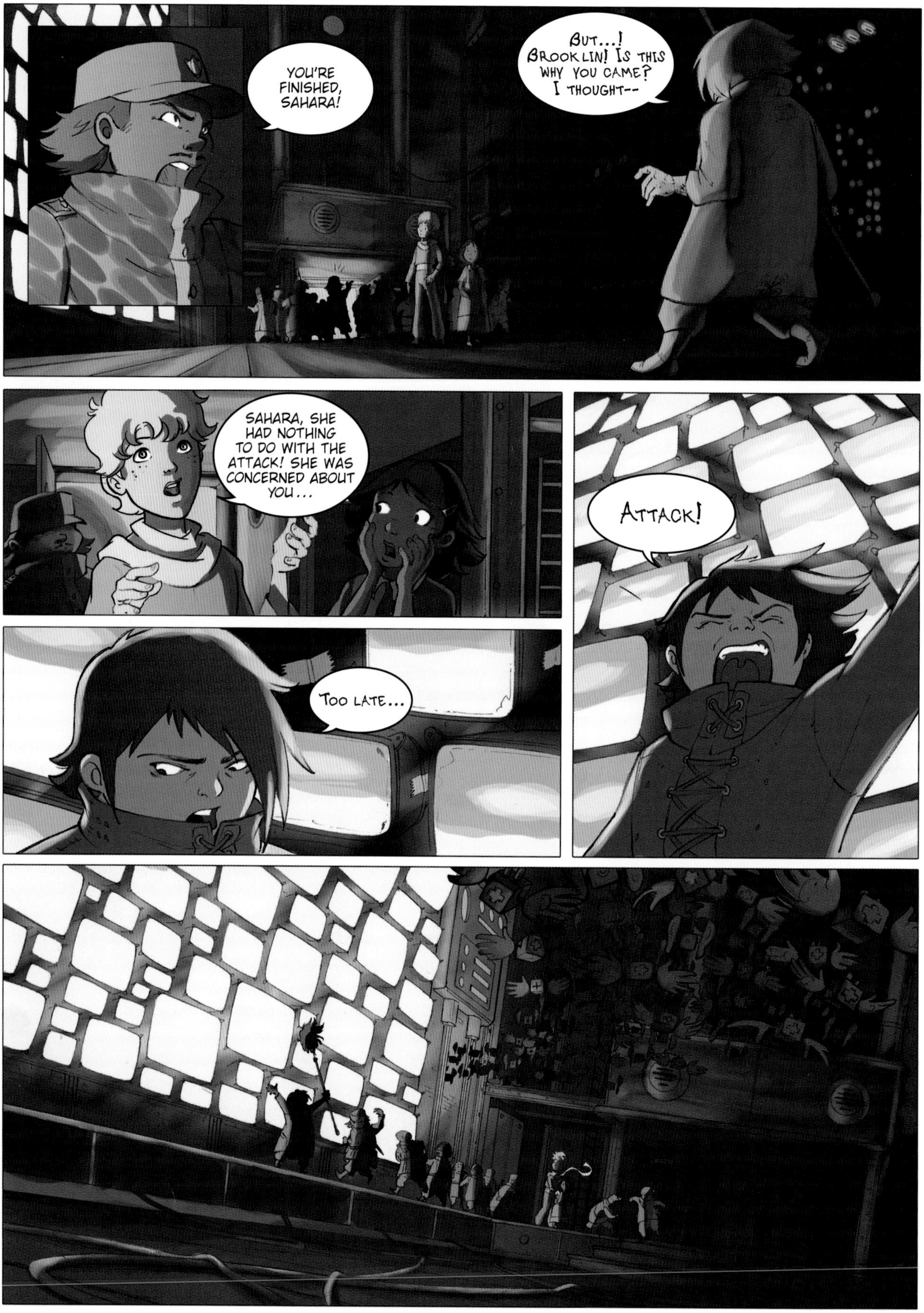

YOU'RE FINISHED, SAHARA!
BUT...! BROOKLIN! IS THIS WHY YOU CAME? I THOUGHT--
SAHARA, SHE HAD NOTHING TO DO WITH THE ATTACK! SHE WAS CONCERNED ABOUT YOU...
TOO LATE...
ATTACK!

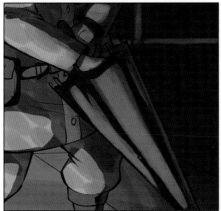

LOOK OUT!

THE WAVELETS!

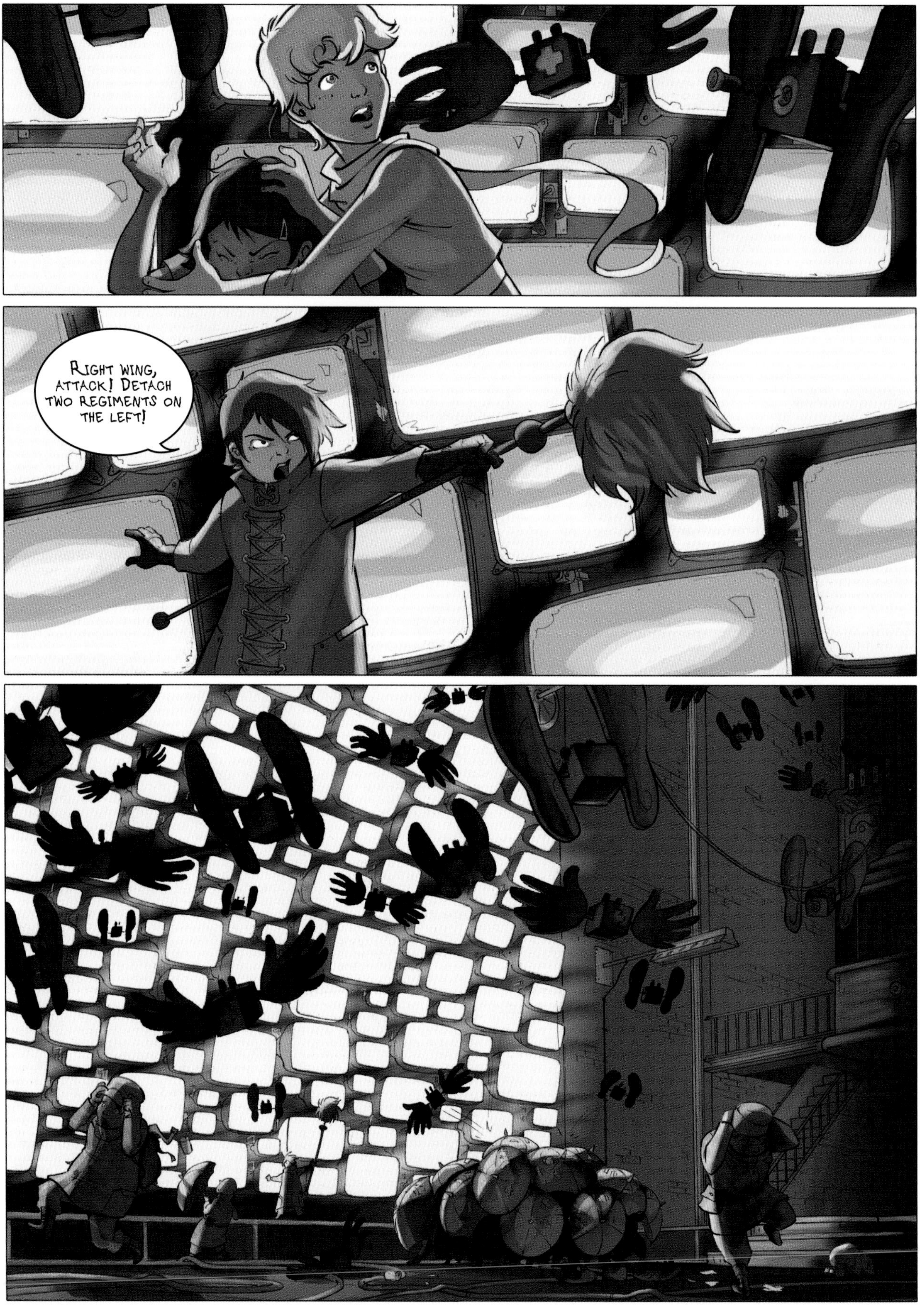
RIGHT WING, ATTACK! DETACH TWO REGIMENTS ON THE LEFT!

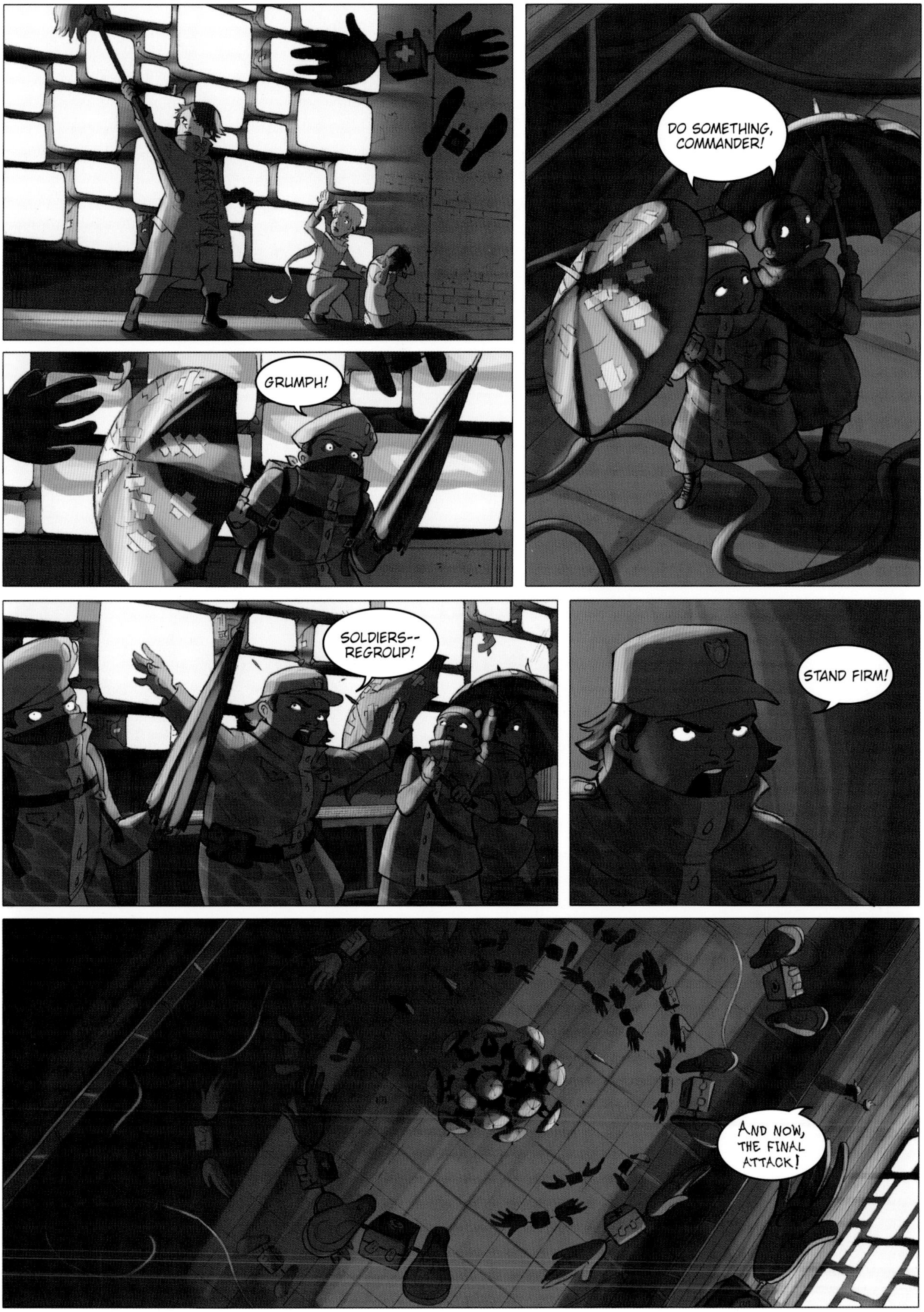
GRUMPH!
DO SOMETHING, COMMANDER!
SOLDIERS-- REGROUP!
STAND FIRM!
AND NOW, THE FINAL ATTACK!

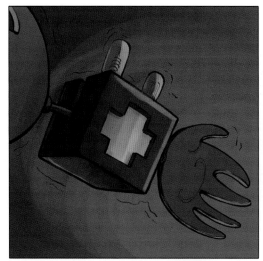

WAIT...
WHAT...?

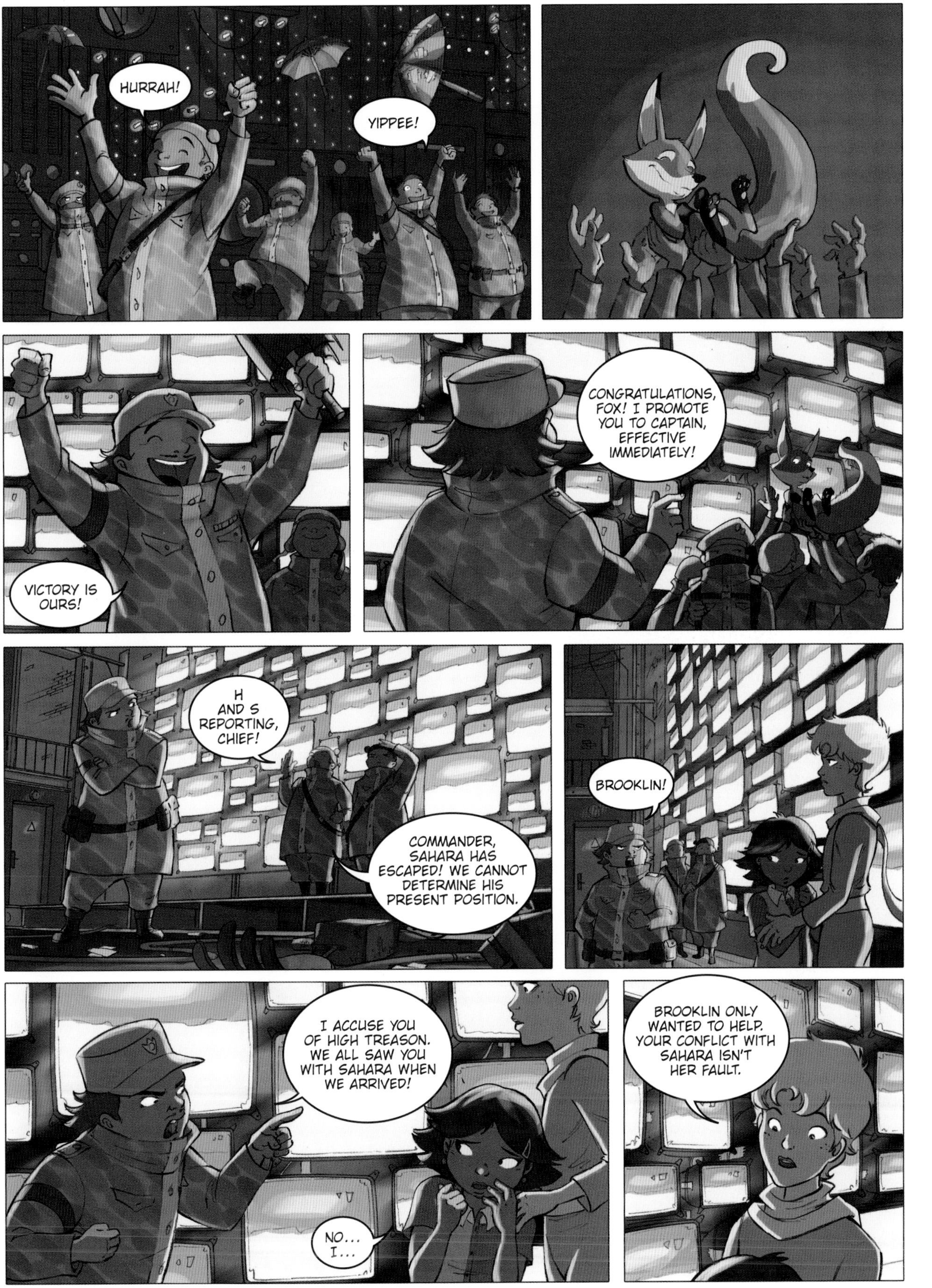
HURRAH!
YIPPEE!
VICTORY IS OURS!
CONGRATULATIONS, FOX! I PROMOTE YOU TO CAPTAIN, EFFECTIVE IMMEDIATELY!
H AND S REPORTING, CHIEF!
COMMANDER, SAHARA HAS ESCAPED! WE CANNOT DETERMINE HIS PRESENT POSITION.
BROOKLIN!
I ACCUSE YOU OF HIGH TREASON. WE ALL SAW YOU WITH SAHARA WHEN WE ARRIVED!
NO... I...
BROOKLIN ONLY WANTED TO HELP. YOUR CONFLICT WITH SAHARA ISN'T HER FAULT.

HOGWASH! GUARDS! PUT THEM BOTH IN IRONS!

SORRY, BAMAKO, BUT I WON'T LET YOU DO THAT!

QUICKLY, BROOKLIN!

WHAT IN THE WORLD...? STOP THEM!

I KNOW WHERE TO FIND SAHARA, LITTLE PRINCE...

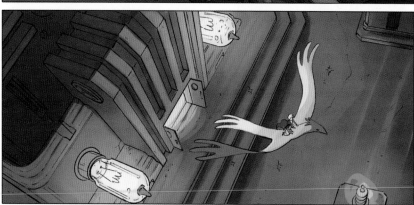

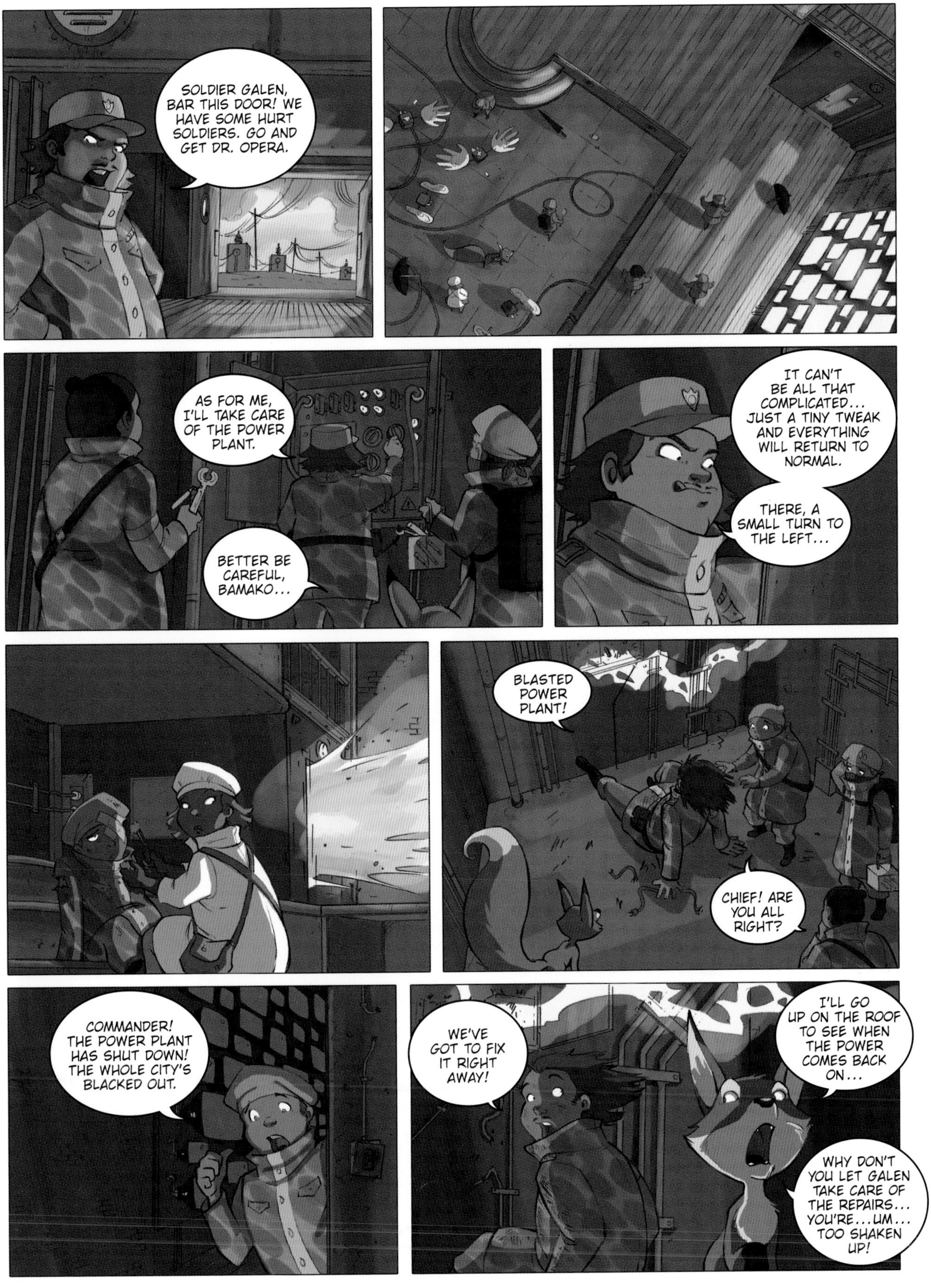
SOLDIER GALEN, BAR THIS DOOR! WE HAVE SOME HURT SOLDIERS. GO AND GET DR. OPERA.
AS FOR ME, I'LL TAKE CARE OF THE POWER PLANT.
BETTER BE CAREFUL, BAMAKO...
IT CAN'T BE ALL THAT COMPLICATED... JUST A TINY TWEAK AND EVERYTHING WILL RETURN TO NORMAL.
THERE, A SMALL TURN TO THE LEFT...
BLASTED POWER PLANT!
CHIEF! ARE YOU ALL RIGHT?
COMMANDER! THE POWER PLANT HAS SHUT DOWN! THE WHOLE CITY'S BLACKED OUT.
WE'VE GOT TO FIX IT RIGHT AWAY!
I'LL GO UP ON THE ROOF TO SEE WHEN THE POWER COMES BACK ON...
WHY DON'T YOU LET GALEN TAKE CARE OF THE REPAIRS... YOU'RE...UM... TOO SHAKEN UP!

PHOOEY! WE'LL BE IN BIG TROUBLE IF POWER ISN'T RESTORED BEFORE NIGHTFALL.

HEY! WHAT'S THAT NOISE?

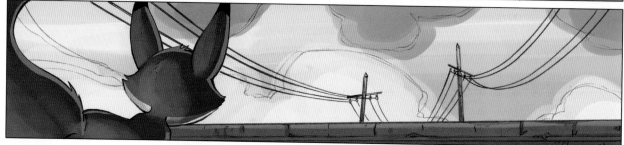

I DON'T GET IT: SAHARA'S BEEN DEFEATED, THE SNAKE HAS LOST--THEY SHOULD BE HAPPY! OF COURSE, THEY STILL CAN'T TALK.

THAT'S IT! THEY NEED ELECTRICITY TO GET THE TAPE OFF THEIR MOUTHS, AND SAHARA'S THE ONLY ONE WHO CAN MAKE THE POWER PLANET WORK.

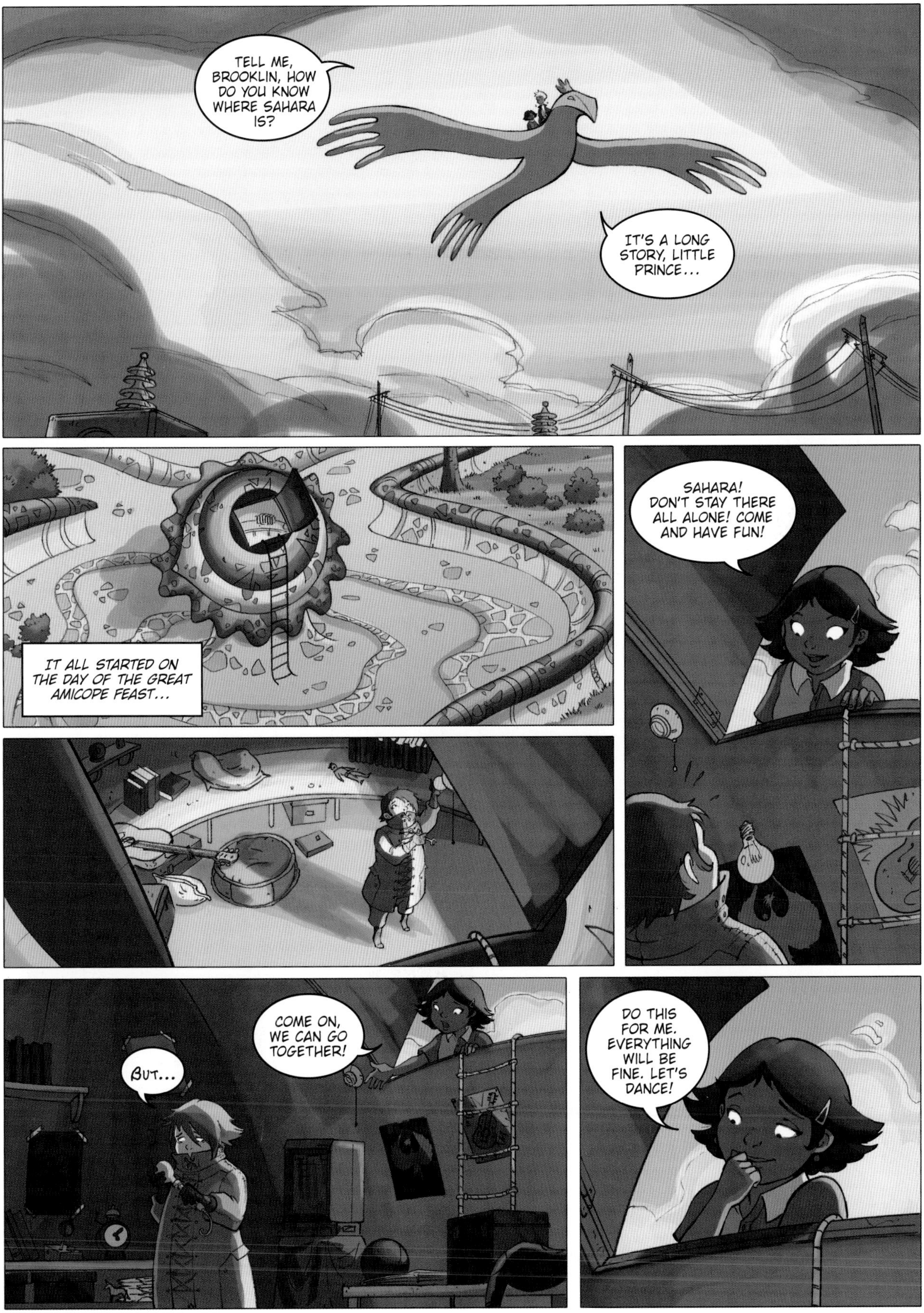
TELL ME, BROOKLIN, HOW DO YOU KNOW WHERE SAHARA IS?
IT'S A LONG STORY, LITTLE PRINCE...
IT ALL STARTED ON THE DAY OF THE GREAT AMICOPE FEAST...
SAHARA! DON'T STAY THERE ALL ALONE! COME AND HAVE FUN!
BUT...
COME ON, WE CAN GO TOGETHER!
DO THIS FOR ME. EVERYTHING WILL BE FINE. LET'S DANCE!

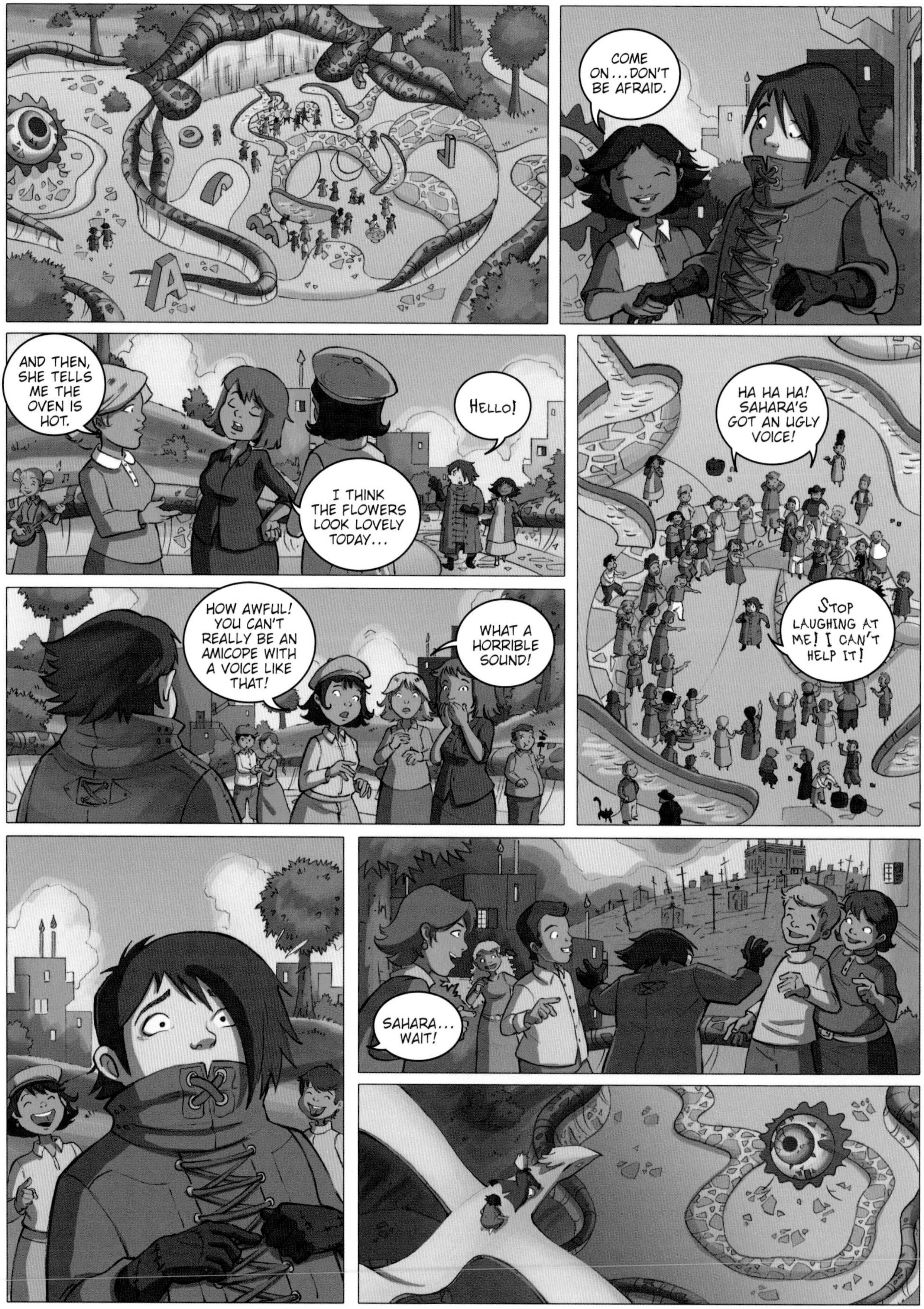
COME ON...DON'T BE AFRAID.
AND THEN, SHE TELLS ME THE OVEN IS HOT.
HELLO!
I THINK THE FLOWERS LOOK LOVELY TODAY...
HA HA HA! SAHARA'S GOT AN UGLY VOICE!
STOP LAUGHING AT ME! I CAN'T HELP IT!
HOW AWFUL! YOU CAN'T REALLY BE AN AMICOPE WITH A VOICE LIKE THAT!
WHAT A HORRIBLE SOUND!
SAHARA... WAIT!

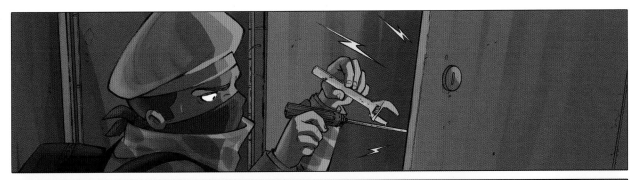

GRUMPH!

SOLDIERS, WE HAVE TO FACE FACTS. WE DON'T KNOW WHAT WE'RE DOING!

COMMANDER BAMAKO, WE NEED SAHARA! ONLY HE CAN REPAIR THE POWER PLANT.

YOU'RE RIGHT, FOX... BUT HOW CAN WE FIND HIM?

MY SENSE OF SMELL, COMMANDER! NO ONE KNOWS THE LITTLE PRINCE'S SCENT BETTER THAN ME, AND HE CAN'T BE FAR FROM SAHARA.

OF COURSE! ANOTHER STROKE OF GENIUS, FOX! ONCE SAHARA HAS REPAIRED THE POWER PLANT, WE CAN GET RID OF HIM.

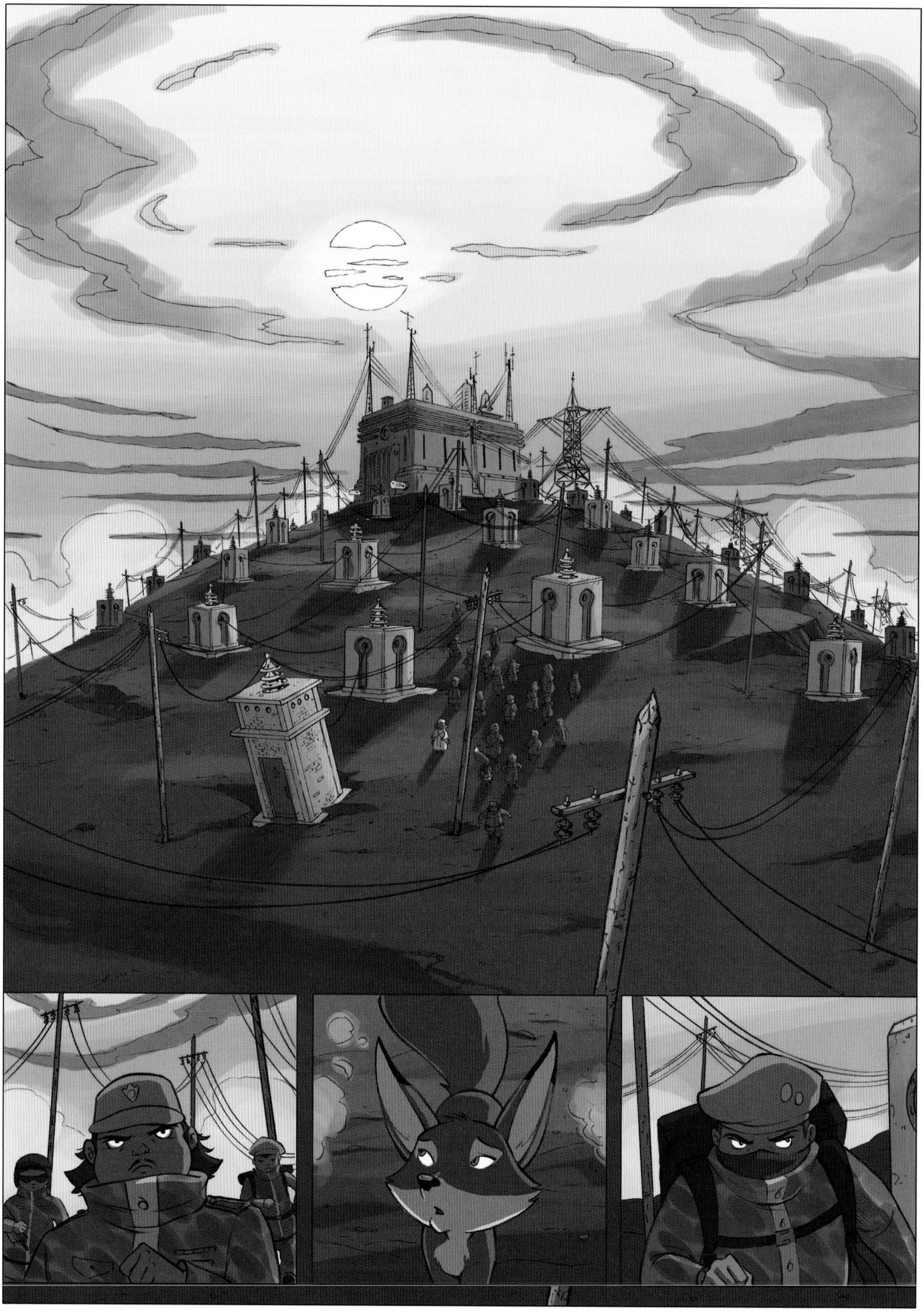

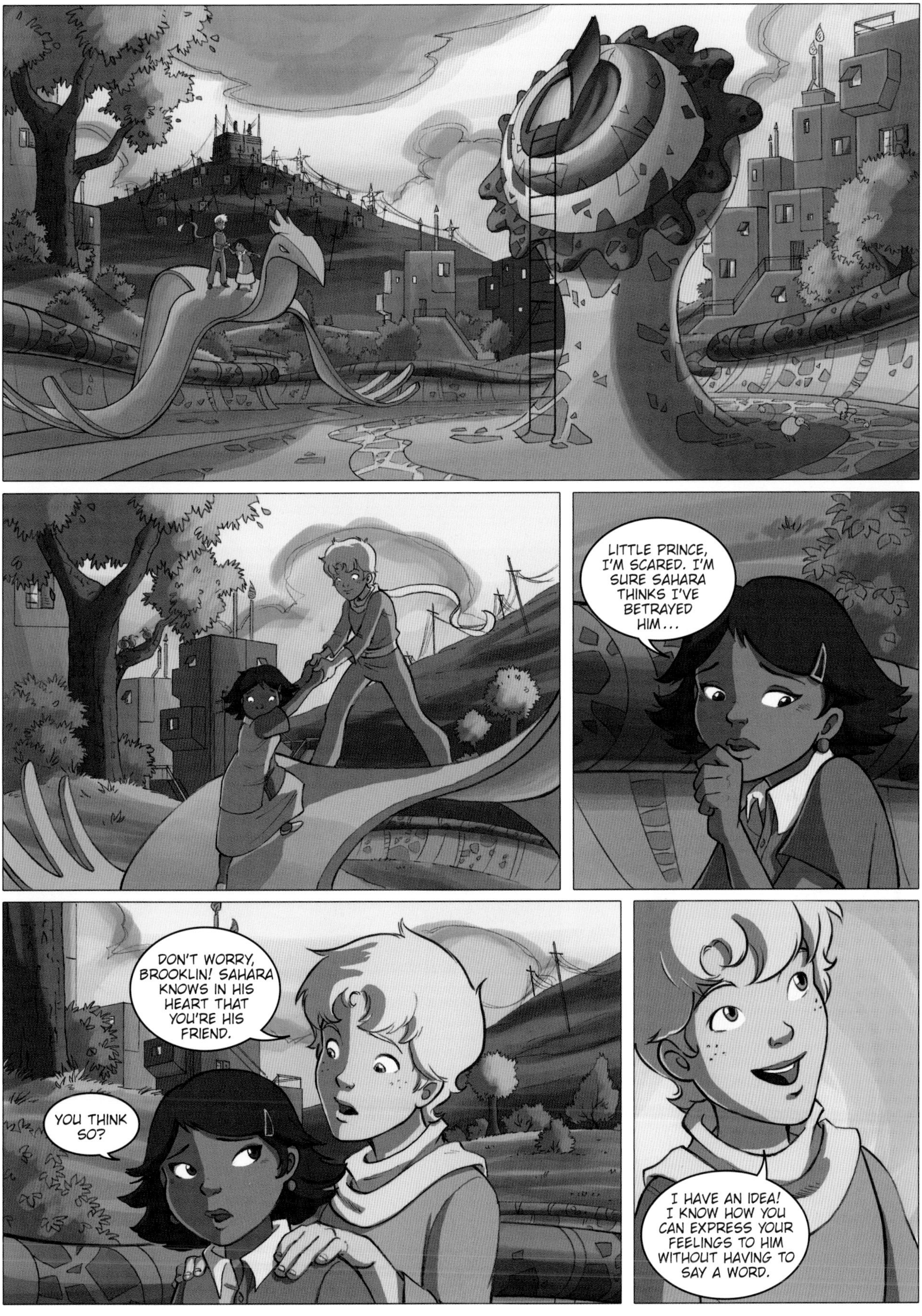

LITTLE PRINCE, I'M SCARED. I'M SURE SAHARA THINKS I'VE BETRAYED HIM...
DON'T WORRY, BROOKLIN! SAHARA KNOWS IN HIS HEART THAT YOU'RE HIS FRIEND.
YOU THINK SO?
I HAVE AN IDEA! I KNOW HOW YOU CAN EXPRESS YOUR FEELINGS TO HIM WITHOUT HAVING TO SAY A WORD.

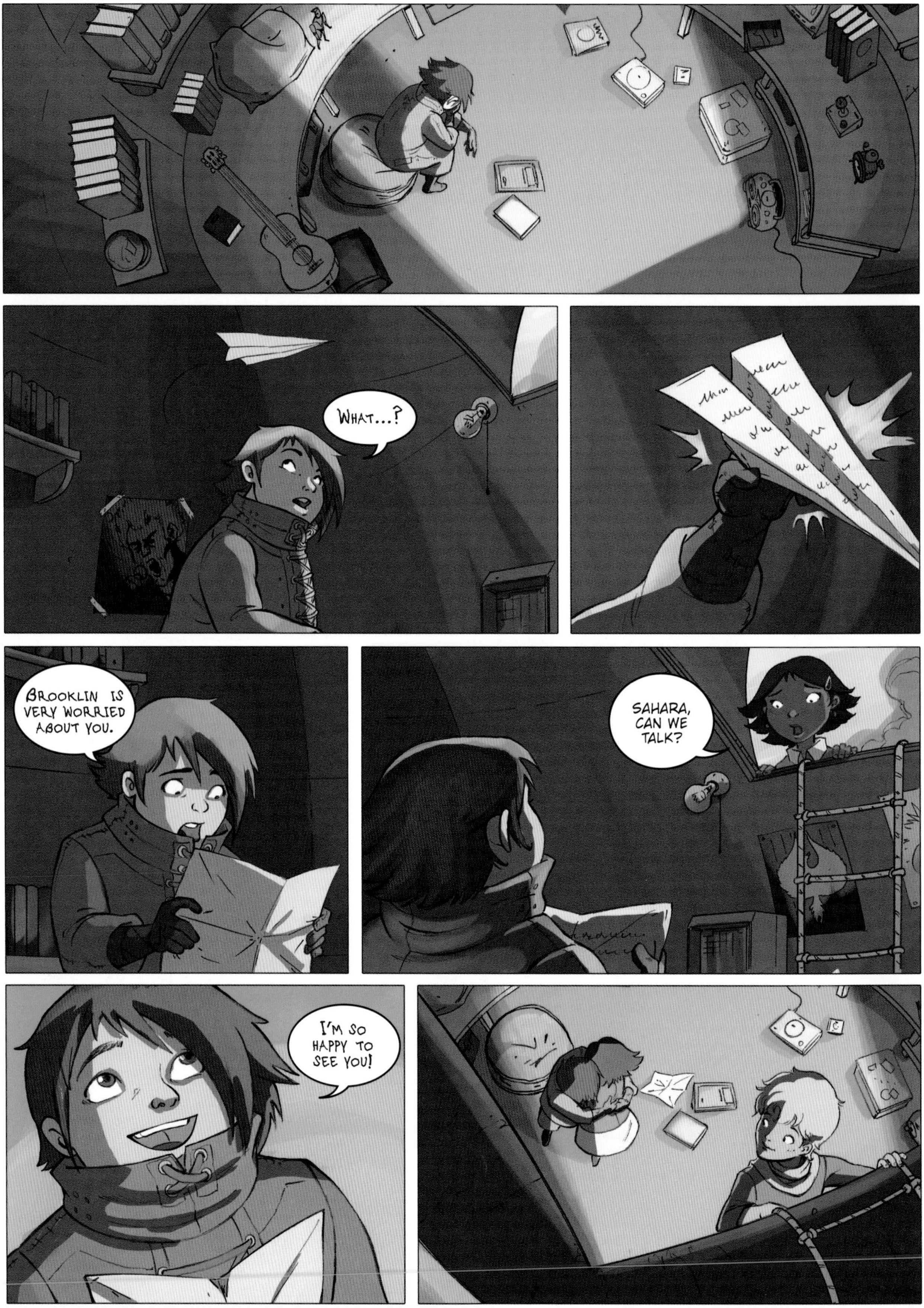
WHAT...?
BROOKLIN IS VERY WORRIED ABOUT YOU.
SAHARA, CAN WE TALK?
I'M SO HAPPY TO SEE YOU!

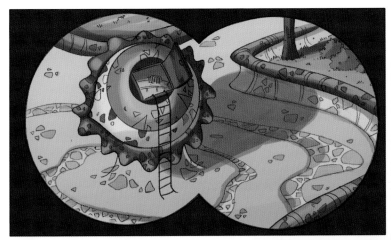

BRAVO! RIGHT AGAIN, FOX! IT'S TIME TO LAUNCH OUR ATTACK AGAINST THE ENEMY.

SOLDIERS, ON TO VICTORY! CHARGE!

BROOKLIN AND I WILL DO EVERYTHING WE CAN TO SET THINGS RIGHT.

IT'S OVER, FILTHY TRAITOR!

NO...WAIT!

YOU WILL COME WITH US AND FIX THE POWER PLANT. THEN, IF YOU'RE LUCKY, YOU'LL SPEND THE REST OF YOUR LIFE IN PRISON!

STAY OUT OF IT, OR YOU'LL SUFFER THE SAME FATE, CIVILIAN LITTLE PRINCE!

COMMANDER BAMAKO, STOP!

COMMANDER, TRUST ME, EVEN IF SAHARA HAS MADE BAD CHOICES, AN EVIL FORCE MANIPULATED HIM... THE SNAKE!

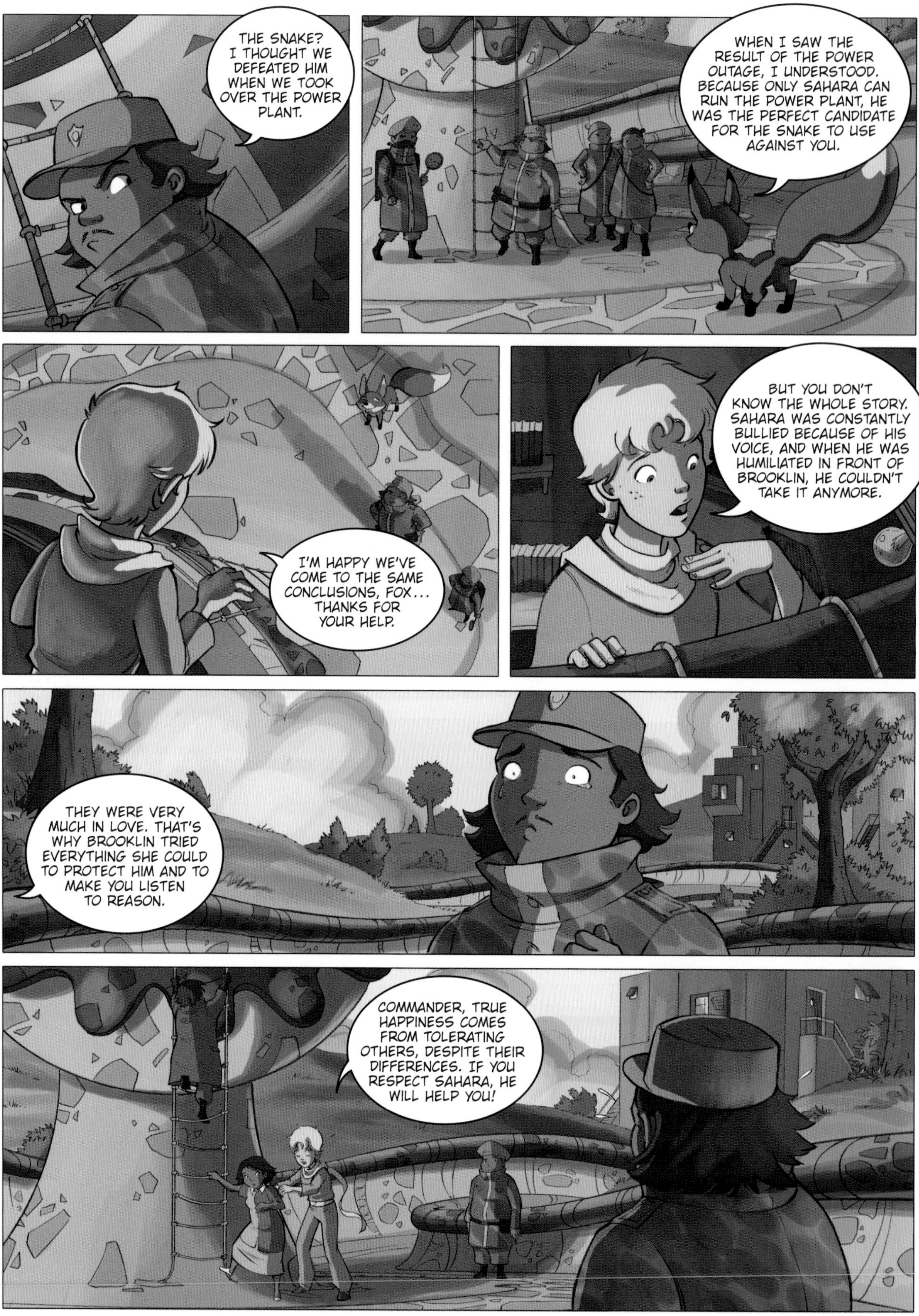

THE SNAKE? I THOUGHT WE DEFEATED HIM WHEN WE TOOK OVER THE POWER PLANT.
WHEN I SAW THE RESULT OF THE POWER OUTAGE, I UNDERSTOOD. BECAUSE ONLY SAHARA CAN RUN THE POWER PLANT, HE WAS THE PERFECT CANDIDATE FOR THE SNAKE TO USE AGAINST YOU.
I'M HAPPY WE'VE COME TO THE SAME CONCLUSIONS, FOX... THANKS FOR YOUR HELP.
BUT YOU DON'T KNOW THE WHOLE STORY. SAHARA WAS CONSTANTLY BULLIED BECAUSE OF HIS VOICE, AND WHEN HE WAS HUMILIATED IN FRONT OF BROOKLIN, HE COULDN'T TAKE IT ANYMORE.
THEY WERE VERY MUCH IN LOVE. THAT'S WHY BROOKLIN TRIED EVERYTHING SHE COULD TO PROTECT HIM AND TO MAKE YOU LISTEN TO REASON.
COMMANDER, TRUE HAPPINESS COMES FROM TOLERATING OTHERS, DESPITE THEIR DIFFERENCES. IF YOU RESPECT SAHARA, HE WILL HELP YOU!

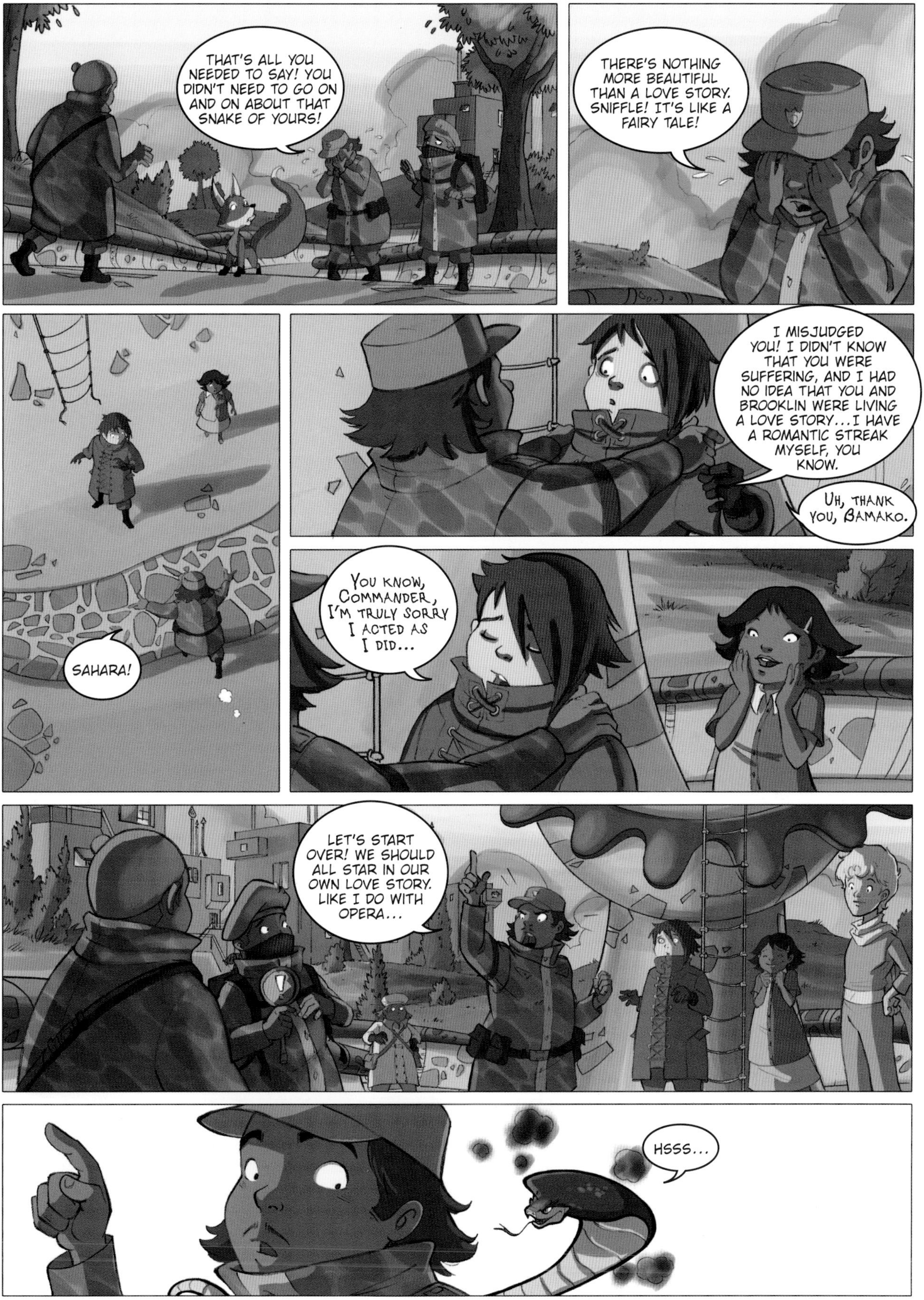

THAT'S ALL YOU NEEDED TO SAY! YOU DIDN'T NEED TO GO ON AND ON ABOUT THAT SNAKE OF YOURS!
THERE'S NOTHING MORE BEAUTIFUL THAN A LOVE STORY. SNIFFLE! IT'S LIKE A FAIRY TALE!
SAHARA!
I MISJUDGED YOU! I DIDN'T KNOW THAT YOU WERE SUFFERING, AND I HAD NO IDEA THAT YOU AND BROOKLIN WERE LIVING A LOVE STORY...I HAVE A ROMANTIC STREAK MYSELF, YOU KNOW.
UH, THANK YOU, BAMAKO.
YOU KNOW, COMMANDER, I'M TRULY SORRY I ACTED AS I DID...
LET'S START OVER! WE SHOULD ALL STAR IN OUR OWN LOVE STORY. LIKE I DO WITH OPERA...
HSSS...

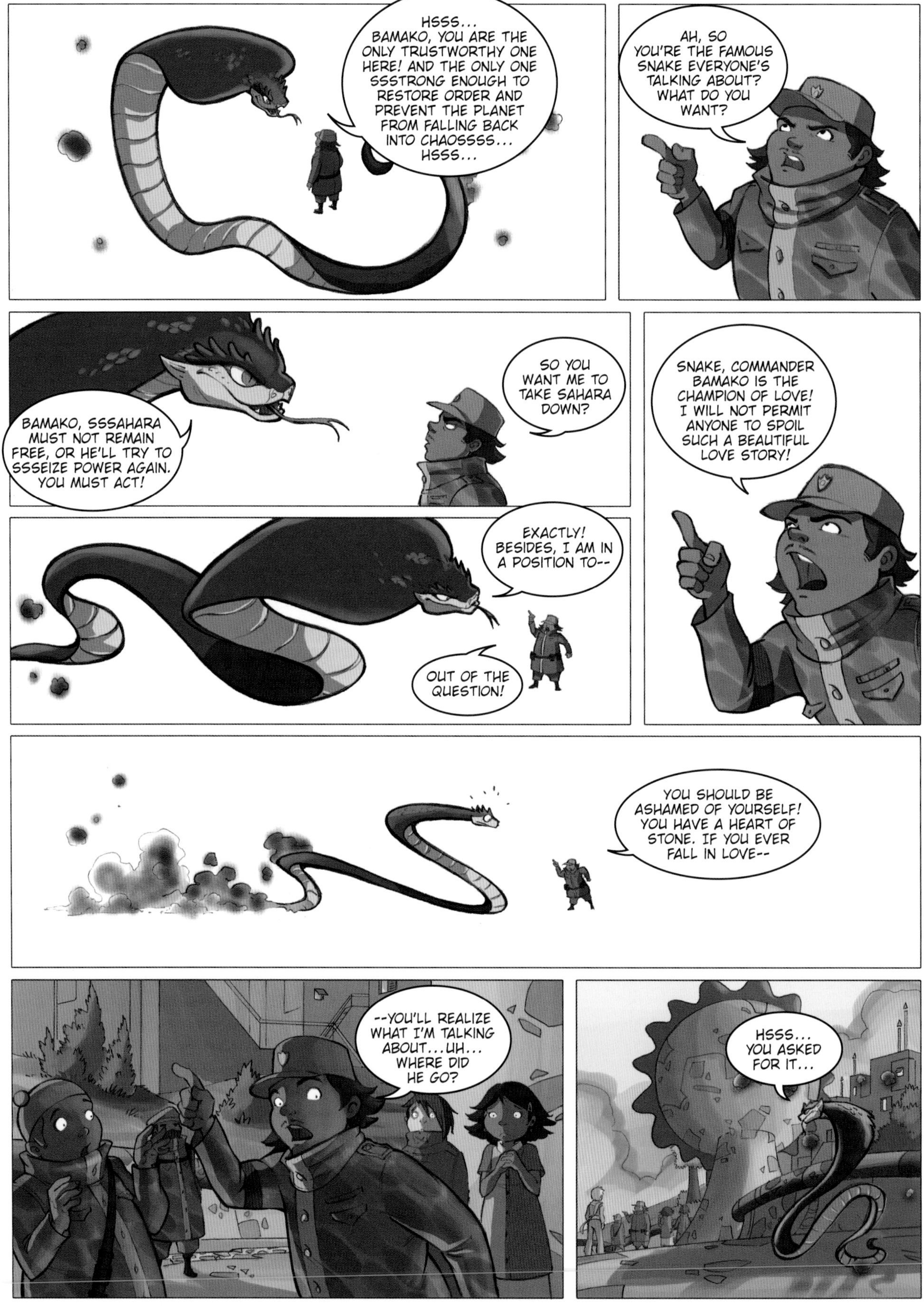
HSSS... BAMAKO, YOU ARE THE ONLY TRUSTWORTHY ONE HERE! AND THE ONLY ONE SSSTRONG ENOUGH TO RESTORE ORDER AND PREVENT THE PLANET FROM FALLING BACK INTO CHAOSSSS... HSSS...
AH, SO YOU'RE THE FAMOUS SNAKE EVERYONE'S TALKING ABOUT? WHAT DO YOU WANT?
BAMAKO, SSSAHARA MUST NOT REMAIN FREE, OR HE'LL TRY TO SSSEIZE POWER AGAIN. YOU MUST ACT!
SO YOU WANT ME TO TAKE SAHARA DOWN?
EXACTLY! BESIDES, I AM IN A POSITION TO--
OUT OF THE QUESTION!
SNAKE, COMMANDER BAMAKO IS THE CHAMPION OF LOVE! I WILL NOT PERMIT ANYONE TO SPOIL SUCH A BEAUTIFUL LOVE STORY!
YOU SHOULD BE ASHAMED OF YOURSELF! YOU HAVE A HEART OF STONE. IF YOU EVER FALL IN LOVE--
--YOU'LL REALIZE WHAT I'M TALKING ABOUT...UH... WHERE DID HE GO?
HSSS... YOU ASKED FOR IT...

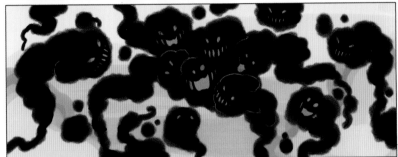

SOLDIERS, FORM UP! PREPARE FOR BATTLE!

NYARK NYARK NYARK!

STOP!

LEAVE SAHARA ALONE! THIS IS BETWEEN YOU AND ME!

LET'S SEE YOU STAND UP AGAINST ROCK PAPER SCISSORS!

ROCK! PAPER! SCISSORS!

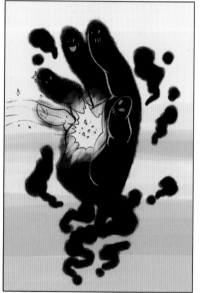

ROCK!

OH NO! PAPER...

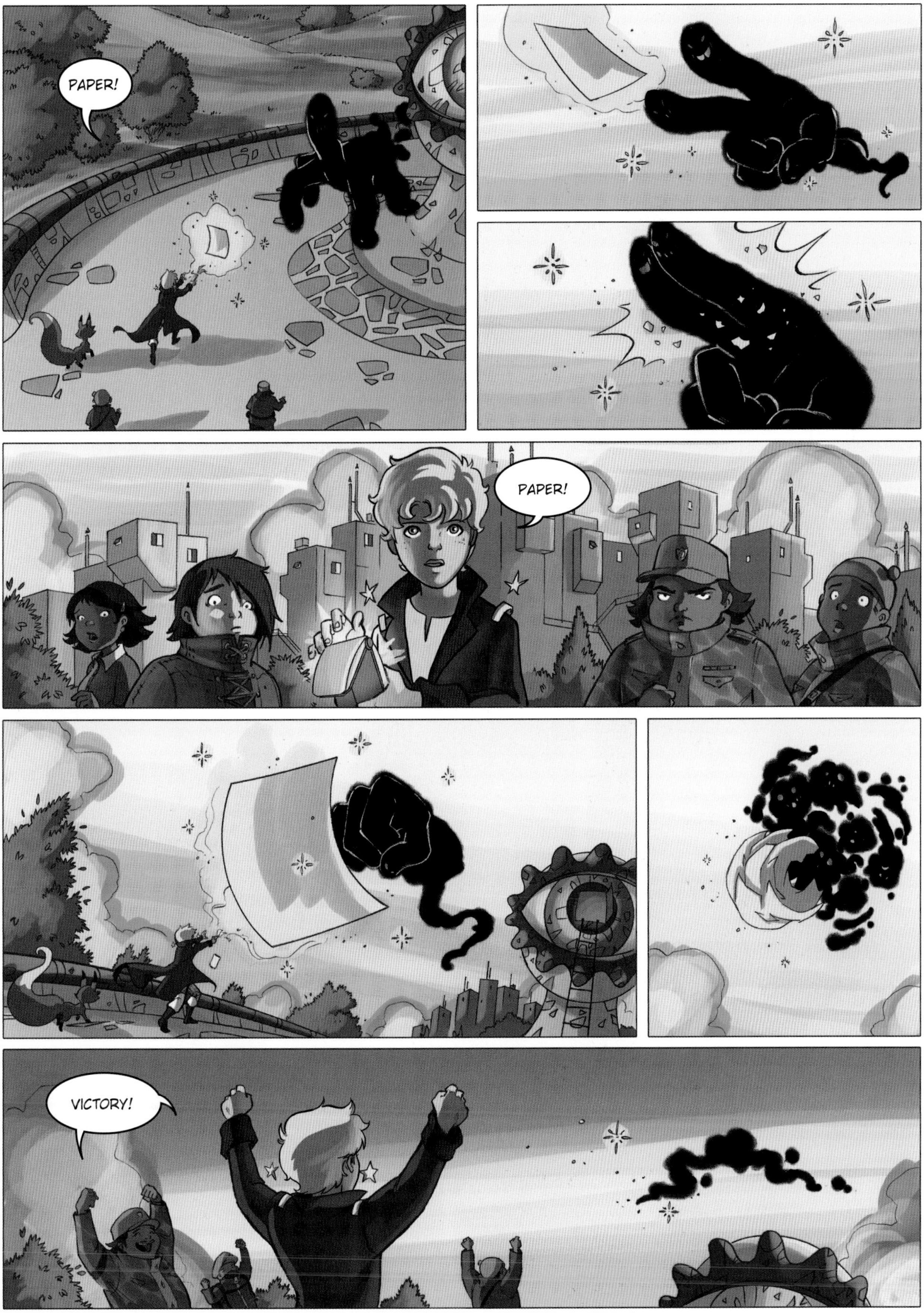
PAPER!
PAPER!
VICTORY!

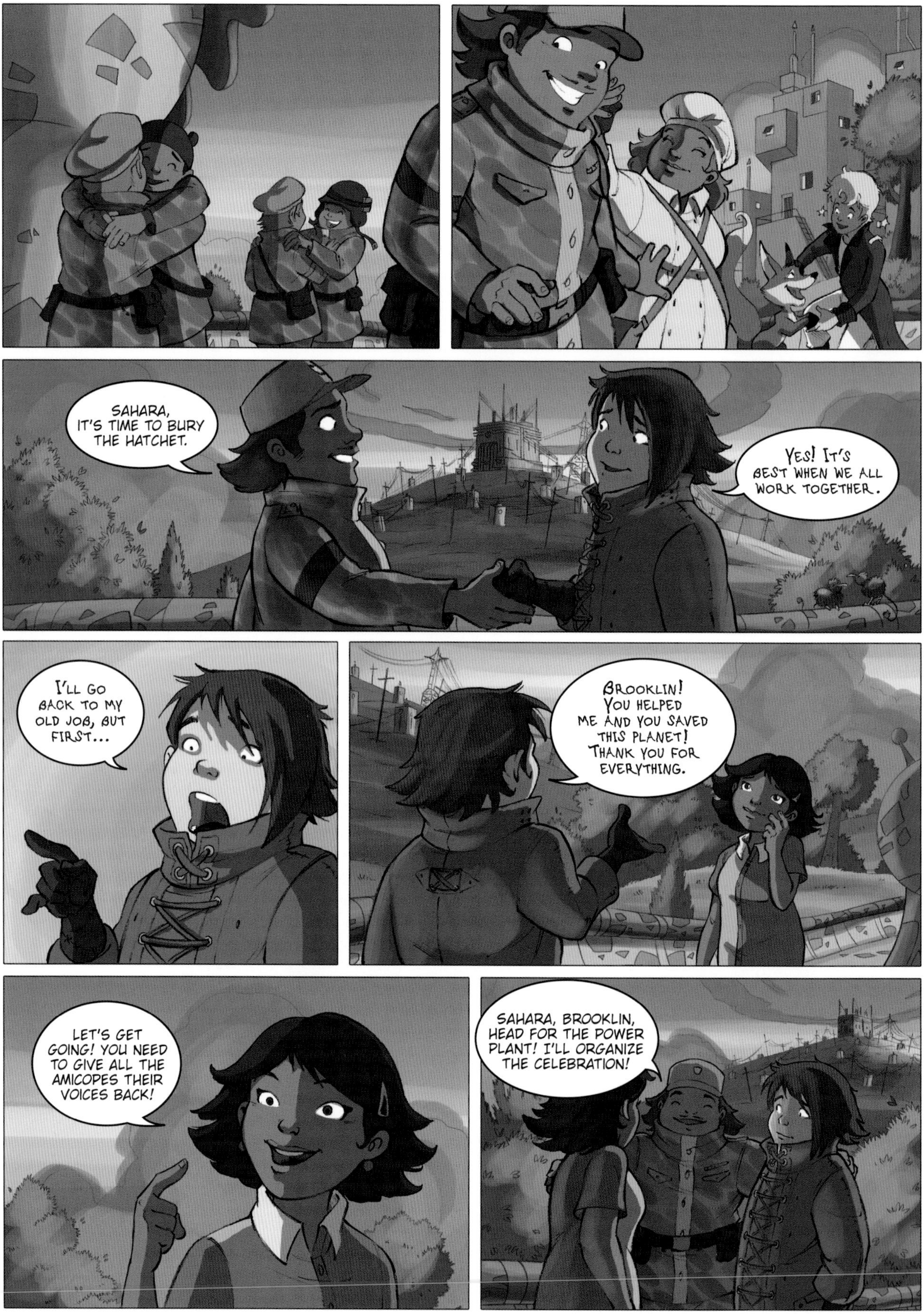
SAHARA, IT'S TIME TO BURY THE HATCHET.
YES! IT'S BEST WHEN WE ALL WORK TOGETHER.
I'LL GO BACK TO MY OLD JOB, BUT FIRST...
BROOKLIN! YOU HELPED ME AND YOU SAVED THIS PLANET! THANK YOU FOR EVERYTHING.
LET'S GET GOING! YOU NEED TO GIVE ALL THE AMICOPES THEIR VOICES BACK!
SAHARA, BROOKLIN, HEAD FOR THE POWER PLANT! I'LL ORGANIZE THE CELEBRATION!

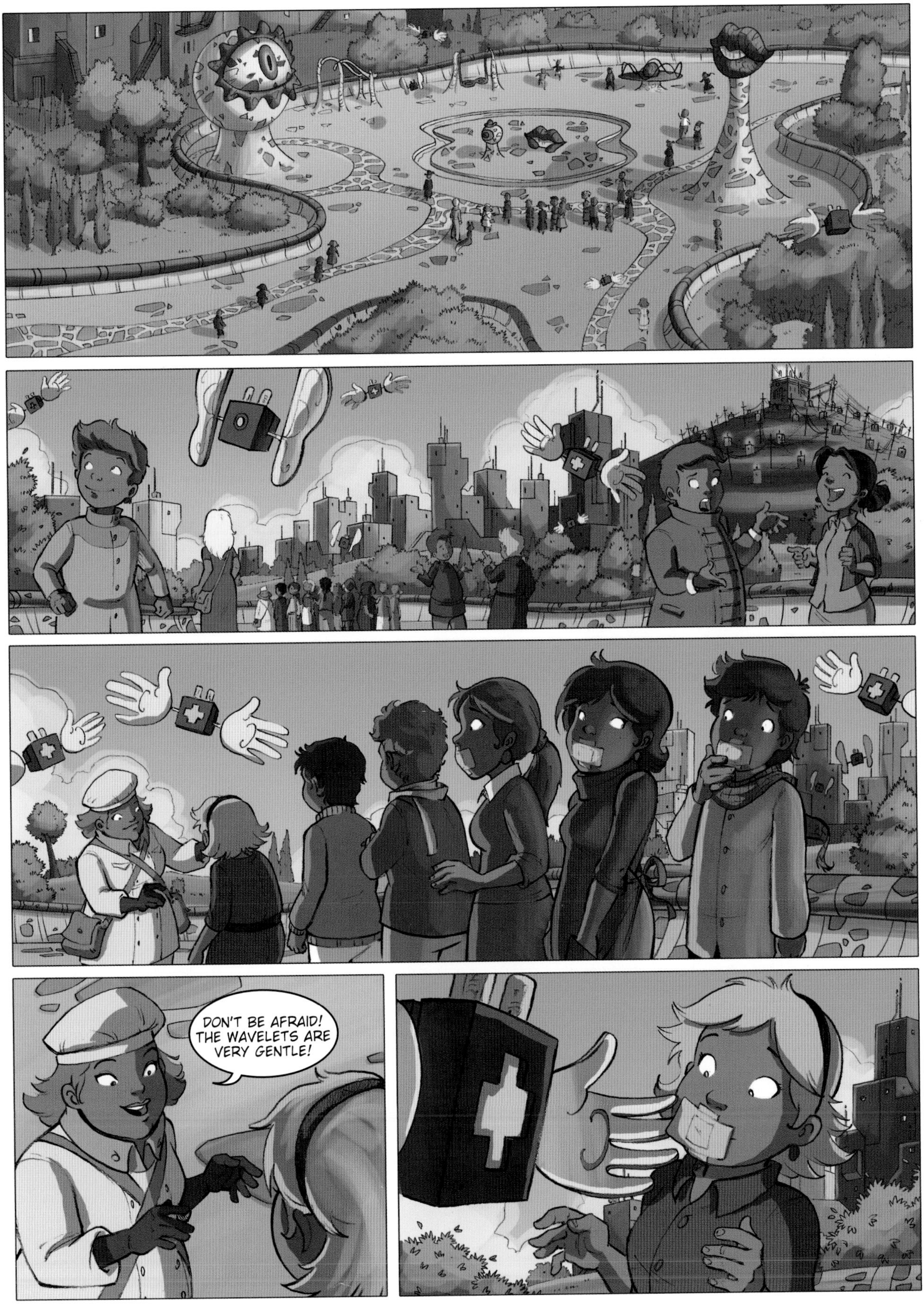
DON'T BE AFRAID! THE WAVELETS ARE VERY GENTLE!

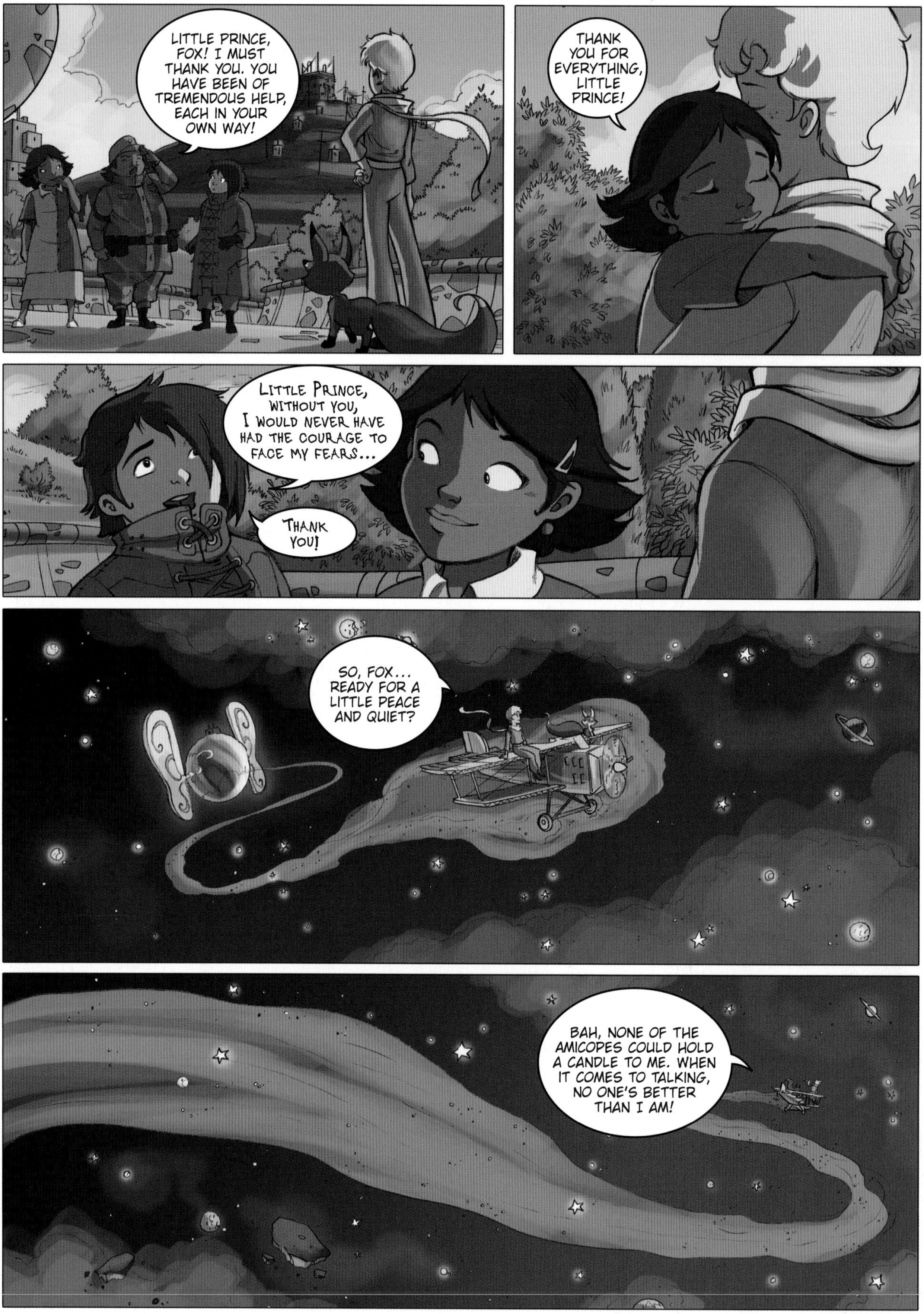

LITTLE PRINCE, FOX! I MUST THANK YOU. YOU HAVE BEEN OF TREMENDOUS HELP, EACH IN YOUR OWN WAY!
THANK YOU FOR EVERYTHING, LITTLE PRINCE!
LITTLE PRINCE, WITHOUT YOU, I WOULD NEVER HAVE HAD THE COURAGE TO FACE MY FEARS...
THANK YOU!
SO, FOX... READY FOR A LITTLE PEACE AND QUIET?
BAH, NONE OF THE AMICOPES COULD HOLD A CANDLE TO ME. WHEN IT COMES TO TALKING, NO ONE'S BETTER THAN I AM!

THE END

The Little Prince

AS IMAGINED BY
JÉRÔME JOUVRAY

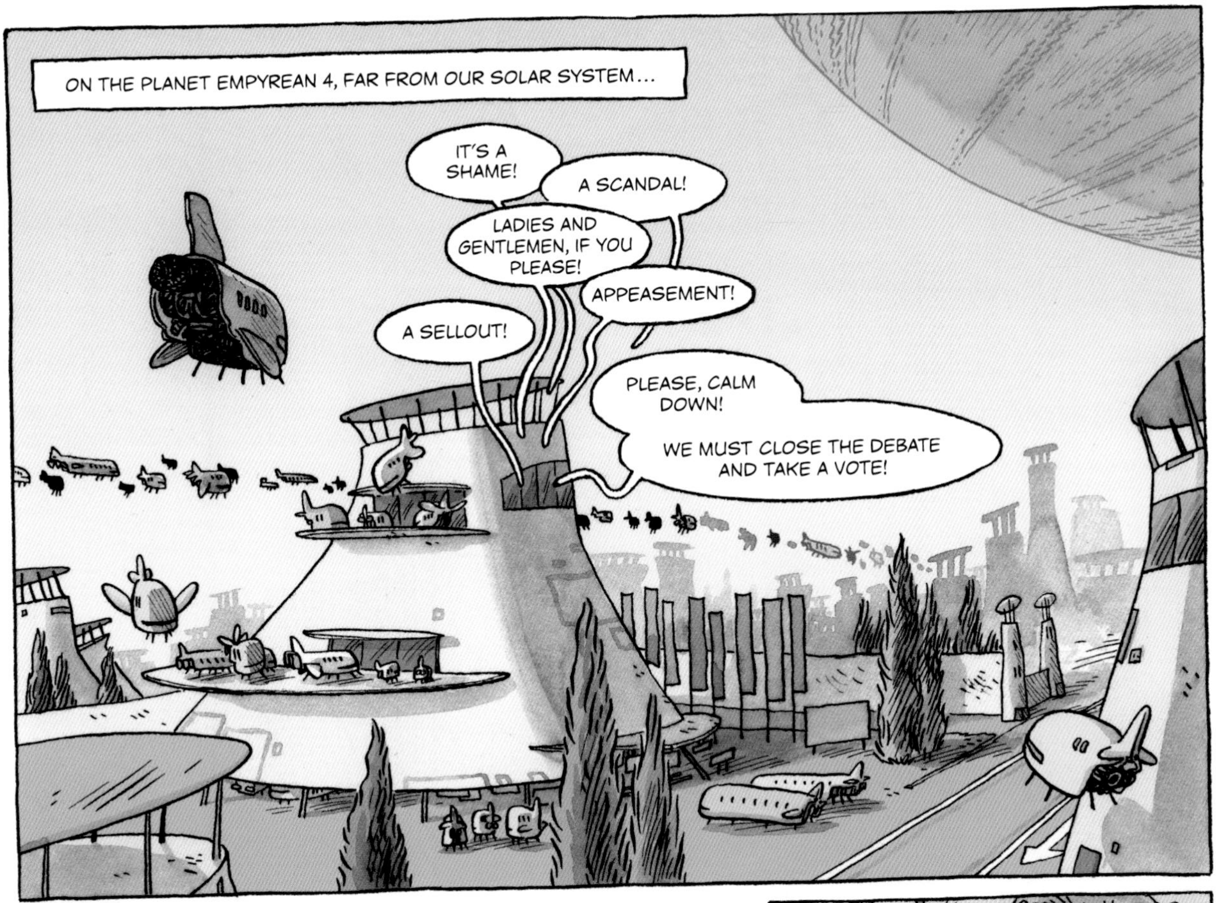
ON THE PLANET EMPYREAN 4, FAR FROM OUR SOLAR SYSTEM...
IT'S A SHAME!
A SCANDAL!
LADIES AND GENTLEMEN, IF YOU PLEASE!
APPEASEMENT!
A SELLOUT!
PLEASE, CALM DOWN!
WE MUST CLOSE THE DEBATE AND TAKE A VOTE!

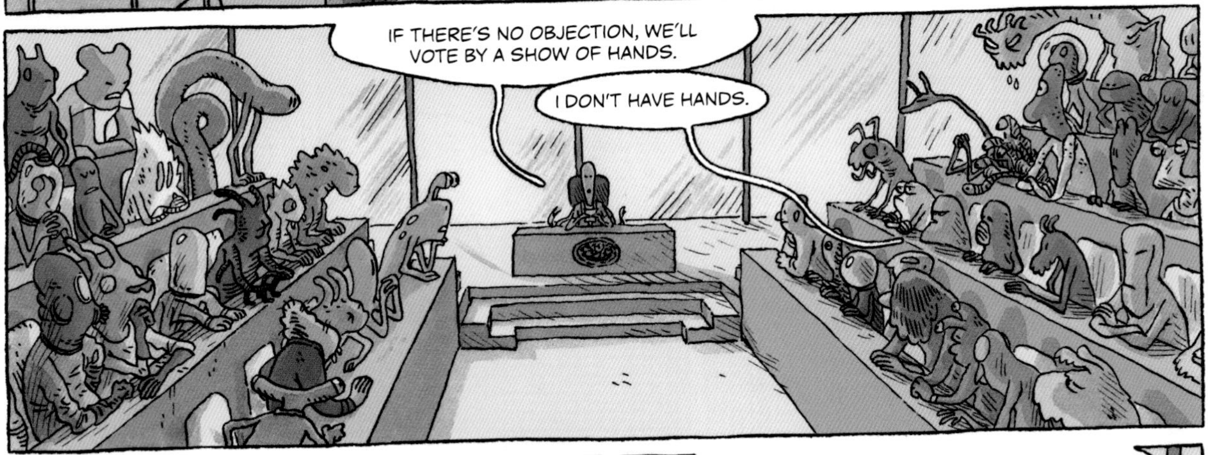
IF THERE'S NO OBJECTION, WE'LL VOTE BY A SHOW OF HANDS.
I DON'T HAVE HANDS.

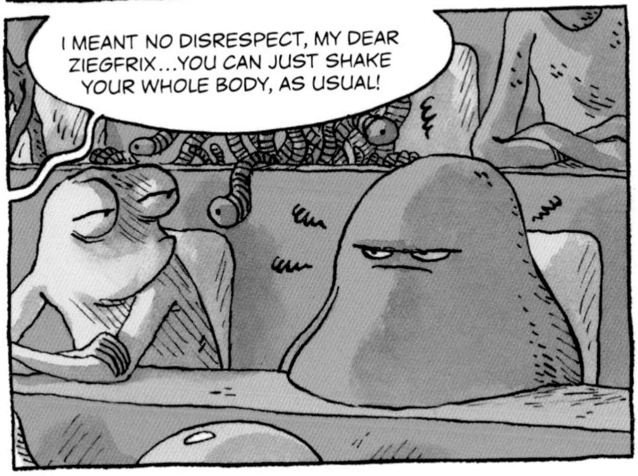
I MEANT NO DISRESPECT, MY DEAR ZIEGFRIX...YOU CAN JUST SHAKE YOUR WHOLE BODY, AS USUAL!

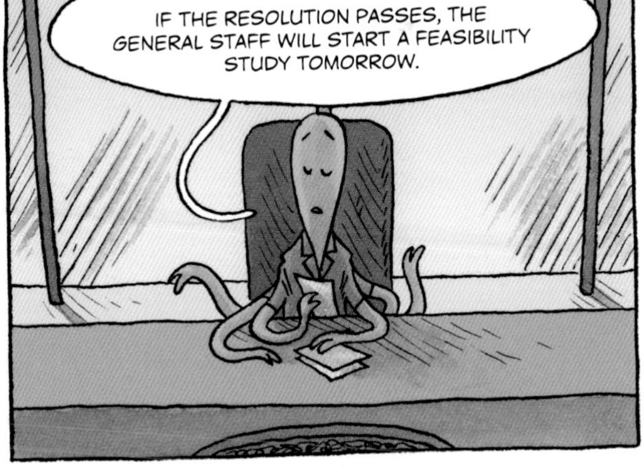
IF THE RESOLUTION PASSES, THE GENERAL STAFF WILL START A FEASIBILITY STUDY TOMORROW.

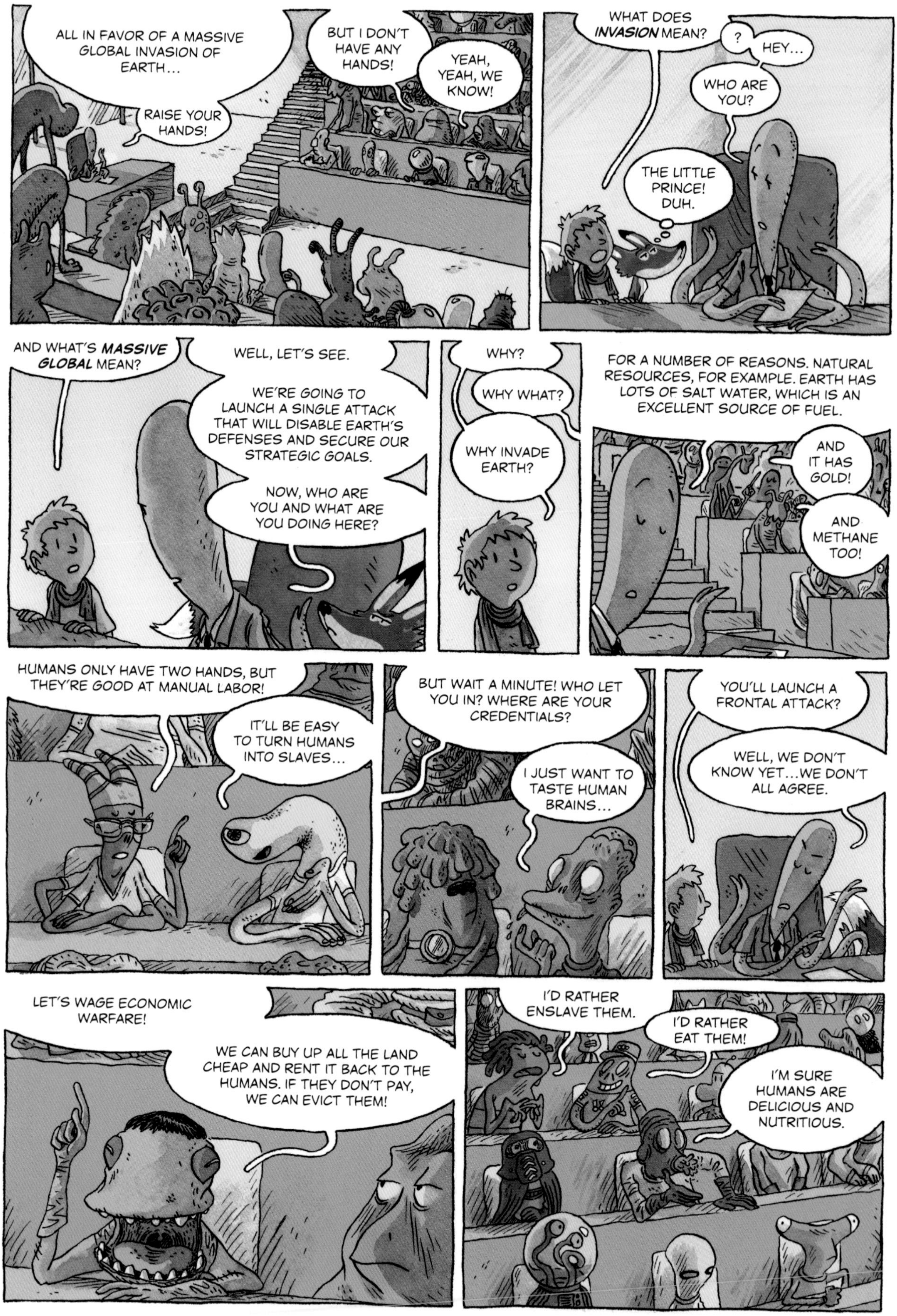
ALL IN FAVOR OF A MASSIVE GLOBAL INVASION OF EARTH...
RAISE YOUR HANDS!
BUT I DON'T HAVE ANY HANDS!
YEAH, YEAH, WE KNOW!
WHAT DOES **INVASION** MEAN?
?
HEY...
WHO ARE YOU?
THE LITTLE PRINCE! DUH.
AND WHAT'S **MASSIVE GLOBAL** MEAN?
WELL, LET'S SEE.
WE'RE GOING TO LAUNCH A SINGLE ATTACK THAT WILL DISABLE EARTH'S DEFENSES AND SECURE OUR STRATEGIC GOALS.
NOW, WHO ARE YOU AND WHAT ARE YOU DOING HERE?
WHY?
WHY WHAT?
WHY INVADE EARTH?
FOR A NUMBER OF REASONS. NATURAL RESOURCES, FOR EXAMPLE. EARTH HAS LOTS OF SALT WATER, WHICH IS AN EXCELLENT SOURCE OF FUEL.
AND IT HAS GOLD!
AND METHANE TOO!
HUMANS ONLY HAVE TWO HANDS, BUT THEY'RE GOOD AT MANUAL LABOR!
IT'LL BE EASY TO TURN HUMANS INTO SLAVES...
BUT WAIT A MINUTE! WHO LET YOU IN? WHERE ARE YOUR CREDENTIALS?
I JUST WANT TO TASTE HUMAN BRAINS...
YOU'LL LAUNCH A FRONTAL ATTACK?
WELL, WE DON'T KNOW YET...WE DON'T ALL AGREE.
LET'S WAGE ECONOMIC WARFARE!
WE CAN BUY UP ALL THE LAND CHEAP AND RENT IT BACK TO THE HUMANS. IF THEY DON'T PAY, WE CAN EVICT THEM!
I'D RATHER ENSLAVE THEM.
I'D RATHER EAT THEM!
I'M SURE HUMANS ARE DELICIOUS AND NUTRITIOUS.

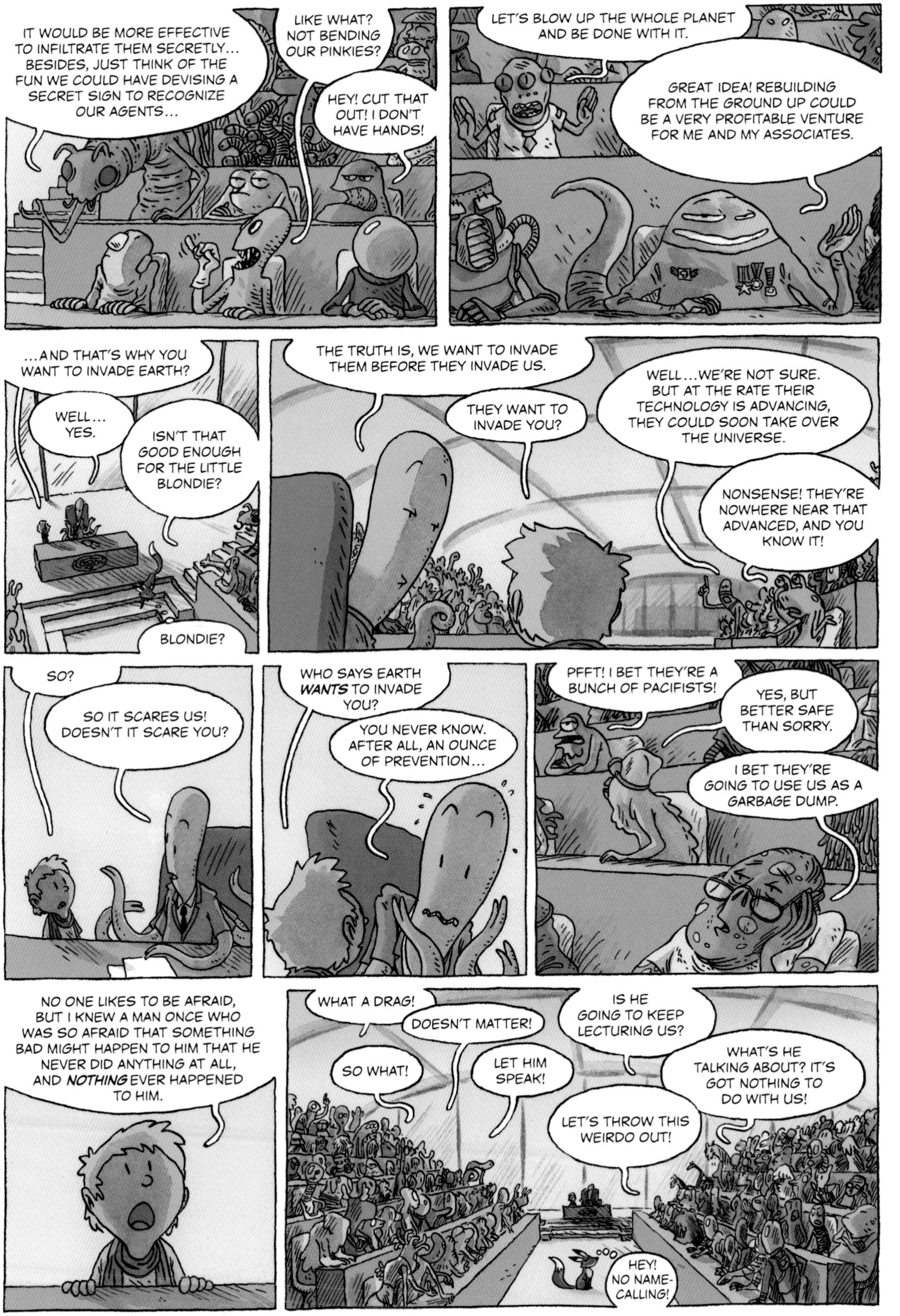
IT WOULD BE MORE EFFECTIVE TO INFILTRATE THEM SECRETLY... BESIDES, JUST THINK OF THE FUN WE COULD HAVE DEVISING A SECRET SIGN TO RECOGNIZE OUR AGENTS...
LIKE WHAT? NOT BENDING OUR PINKIES?
HEY! CUT THAT OUT! I DON'T HAVE HANDS!
LET'S BLOW UP THE WHOLE PLANET AND BE DONE WITH IT.
GREAT IDEA! REBUILDING FROM THE GROUND UP COULD BE A VERY PROFITABLE VENTURE FOR ME AND MY ASSOCIATES.
...AND THAT'S WHY YOU WANT TO INVADE EARTH?
WELL... YES.
ISN'T THAT GOOD ENOUGH FOR THE LITTLE BLONDIE?
BLONDIE?
THE TRUTH IS, WE WANT TO INVADE THEM BEFORE THEY INVADE US.
THEY WANT TO INVADE YOU?
WELL...WE'RE NOT SURE. BUT AT THE RATE THEIR TECHNOLOGY IS ADVANCING, THEY COULD SOON TAKE OVER THE UNIVERSE.
NONSENSE! THEY'RE NOWHERE NEAR THAT ADVANCED, AND YOU KNOW IT!
SO?
SO IT SCARES US! DOESN'T IT SCARE YOU?
WHO SAYS EARTH *WANTS* TO INVADE YOU?
YOU NEVER KNOW. AFTER ALL, AN OUNCE OF PREVENTION...
PFFT! I BET THEY'RE A BUNCH OF PACIFISTS!
YES, BUT BETTER SAFE THAN SORRY.
I BET THEY'RE GOING TO USE US AS A GARBAGE DUMP.
NO ONE LIKES TO BE AFRAID, BUT I KNEW A MAN ONCE WHO WAS SO AFRAID THAT SOMETHING BAD MIGHT HAPPEN TO HIM THAT HE NEVER DID ANYTHING AT ALL, AND *NOTHING* EVER HAPPENED TO HIM.
WHAT A DRAG!
DOESN'T MATTER!
SO WHAT!
LET HIM SPEAK!
IS HE GOING TO KEEP LECTURING US?
WHAT'S HE TALKING ABOUT? IT'S GOT NOTHING TO DO WITH US!
LET'S THROW THIS WEIRDO OUT!
HEY! NO NAME-CALLING!

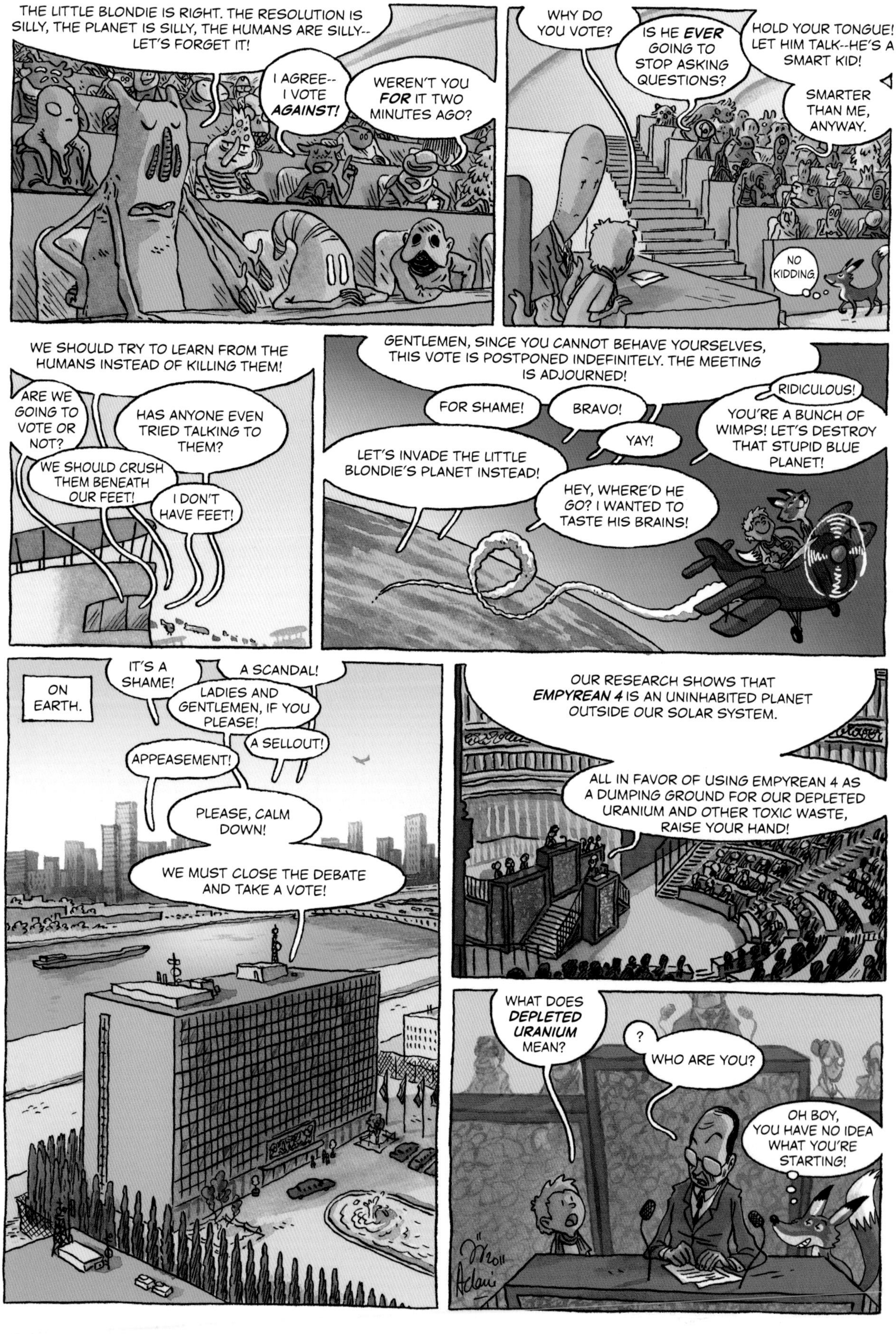
THE LITTLE BLONDIE IS RIGHT. THE RESOLUTION IS SILLY, THE PLANET IS SILLY, THE HUMANS ARE SILLY--LET'S FORGET IT!
I AGREE--I VOTE *AGAINST!*
WEREN'T YOU *FOR* IT TWO MINUTES AGO?
WHY DO YOU VOTE?
IS HE *EVER* GOING TO STOP ASKING QUESTIONS?
HOLD YOUR TONGUE! LET HIM TALK--HE'S A SMART KID!
SMARTER THAN ME, ANYWAY.
NO KIDDING.
WE SHOULD TRY TO LEARN FROM THE HUMANS INSTEAD OF KILLING THEM!
ARE WE GOING TO VOTE OR NOT?
HAS ANYONE EVEN TRIED TALKING TO THEM?
WE SHOULD CRUSH THEM BENEATH OUR FEET!
I DON'T HAVE FEET!
GENTLEMEN, SINCE YOU CANNOT BEHAVE YOURSELVES, THIS VOTE IS POSTPONED INDEFINITELY. THE MEETING IS ADJOURNED!
FOR SHAME!
BRAVO!
RIDICULOUS!
YOU'RE A BUNCH OF WIMPS! LET'S DESTROY THAT STUPID BLUE PLANET!
YAY!
LET'S INVADE THE LITTLE BLONDIE'S PLANET INSTEAD!
HEY, WHERE'D HE GO? I WANTED TO TASTE HIS BRAINS!
ON EARTH.
IT'S A SHAME!
A SCANDAL!
LADIES AND GENTLEMEN, IF YOU PLEASE!
A SELLOUT!
APPEASEMENT!
PLEASE, CALM DOWN!
WE MUST CLOSE THE DEBATE AND TAKE A VOTE!
OUR RESEARCH SHOWS THAT *EMPYREAN 4* IS AN UNINHABITED PLANET OUTSIDE OUR SOLAR SYSTEM.
ALL IN FAVOR OF USING EMPYREAN 4 AS A DUMPING GROUND FOR OUR DEPLETED URANIUM AND OTHER TOXIC WASTE, RAISE YOUR HAND!
WHAT DOES *DEPLETED URANIUM* MEAN?
?
WHO ARE YOU?
OH BOY, YOU HAVE NO IDEA WHAT YOU'RE STARTING!

ANTOINE DE SAINT-EXUPÉRY
Aviator • Author • Adventurer • Hero

Antoine de Saint-Exupéry, author of the novel *The Little Prince* on which these new adventures are based, was born on June 29, 1900, in Lyon, France. He was the third of five children: Marie-Madeleine, Simone, Antoine, François, and Gabrielle. It was when he was twelve years old, during his summer break from boarding school, that airplanes and flying first made a huge impression on him.

In 1920, he was accepted into the École des Beaux-Arts in Paris to study architecture, but the next year he joined the Second Aviation Regiment of the armed forces and received his pilot's license. In 1922, he had his first plane crash and suffered a head fracture. He had to leave the armed forces and work at different jobs on the ground to earn a living.

By May of 1926, Saint-Exupéry was able to fly again. He delivered airmail, which was a new and sometimes dangerous profession, on routes from France to Senegal and all the way to South America. That was where, in 1931, he met and married Consuelo Suncin.

From 1933 to 1938, Saint-Exupéry was very busy. He traveled to North Africa and Indochina and attempted to break the flight speed record from Paris to Saigon, Vietnam—during which his plane crashed again. It went down in the middle of the Sahara Desert. After his recovery, his life became even busier. He wrote newspaper reports in Spain on the Spanish Civil War, scouted airplane routes between Casablanca and Timbuktu, wrote a screenplay, registered several patents, and traveled to the United States. In 1939, with the start of World War II, he returned to France and talked his way into a job as a high-risk reconnaissance pilot for the French Air Force. But this only lasted until France reached an armistice agreement with Germany.

In December 1940, Saint-Exupéry returned to visit friends in New York, where he finally began work on *The Little Prince*. The story is narrated by a pilot who has crashed his plane into the Sahara Desert. He meets a little prince visiting from a faraway asteroid. Along the way, the prince also meets Fox and Snake. By late 1942, after spending the spring and summer writing and illustrating, Saint-Exupéry had completed his novel, and in April 1943 it was published in his native language of French *(Le Petit Prince)* and in English.

Saint-Exupéry was eager to return to the war. He decided to join the Free French Forces in Algeria, who were continuing the fight against the Axis powers. Because of his age, at first he had a hard time convincing them to let him fly. He was authorized to fly five dangerous missions. In fact, he flew eight. On July 31, 1944, Saint-Exupéry went on a scouting flight to prepare for military landings in the south of France. His plane disappeared over the water, and he was never seen again.

Over the decades since *The Little Prince* was published, it has gone on to become one of the best-selling novels of all time. In 2003, a small moon in our solar system's asteroid belt was named Petit-Prince in honor of the masterpiece Saint-Exupéry created.

THE LITTLE PRINCE IN THE TWENTY-FIRST CENTURY

The Little Prince is a landmark of literature and one of the most translated and beloved books in the world. It tackles universal topics with a unique philosophical and poetic sensibility. Sixty-five years after the first edition, the Saint-Exupéry Estate decided to bring the character back for a whole new generation . . . and for everyone who has ever loved the boy who sees the world with his heart.

The Little Prince now returns in a series of new adventures that remain true to the spirit of the original work. He will travel from planet to planet chasing the wicked Snake, who wants to plunge the whole universe into darkness. On each planet, the Snake sends bad thoughts into the minds of its inhabitants, making them sad and grim, draining the life out of their planet. The Little Prince must leave his beautiful Rose behind and must use his vision and courage to defeat the Snake, bringing along his friend Fox to save planets in danger across the universe.

ABOUT THE ADAPTERS

After several years in video games and Japanese animation, adapter Guillaume Dorison became literary editor for the publisher Les Humanoïdes Associés in 2006, where he launched the Shogun Collection dedicated to original manga. In June 2010, he founded Élyum Studio with Didier Poli, Jean-Baptiste Hostache, and Xavier Dorison to provide services for the creation of graphic novels. In addition to his position as director of writing for Élyum Studio, he has more than two dozen comics and manga to his credit under the pseudonym IZU, has written several titles in the Explora series on world explorers for French publisher Glénat, and won the 2010 Animeland Prize for best French manga.

Didier Poli, artistic director for the new graphic novel adaptations based on The Little Prince, was born in Lyon in 1971. After graduate studies in applied arts, he worked for various animation studios including Disney. He was working as artistic director for the video game company Kalisto Entertainment when he met Manuel Bichebois in 2001 and began drawing Bichebois's graphic novel series L'Enfant de l'orage. At the 2004 Nîmes Festival, Didier Poli received the Bronze Boar prize for young talent. He continues, along with his work on graphic novels, to work regularly in cartoons and video games as a designer and storyboard artist.

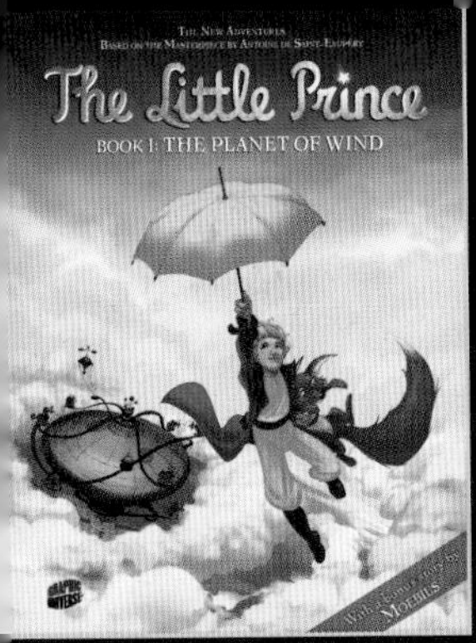
The Little Prince
BOOK 1: THE PLANET OF WIND
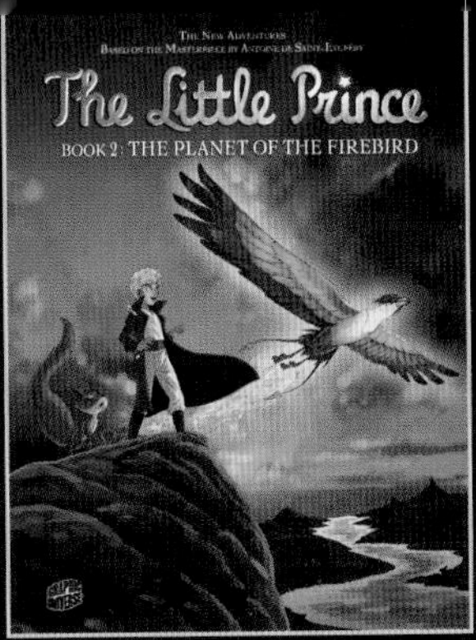
The Little Prince
BOOK 2: THE PLANET OF THE FIREBIRD
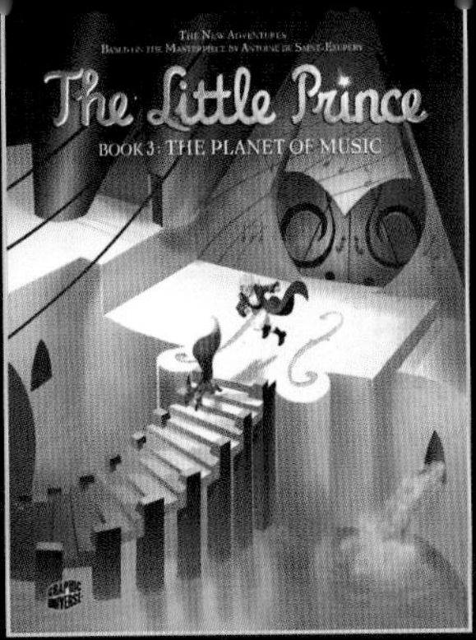
The Little Prince
BOOK 3: THE PLANET OF MUSIC
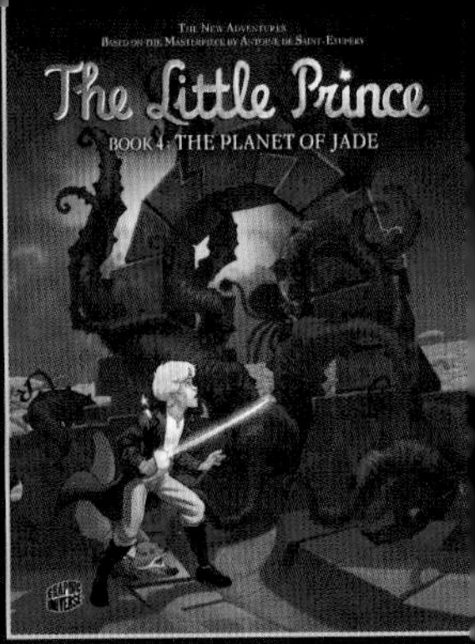
The Little Prince
BOOK 4: THE PLANET OF JADE
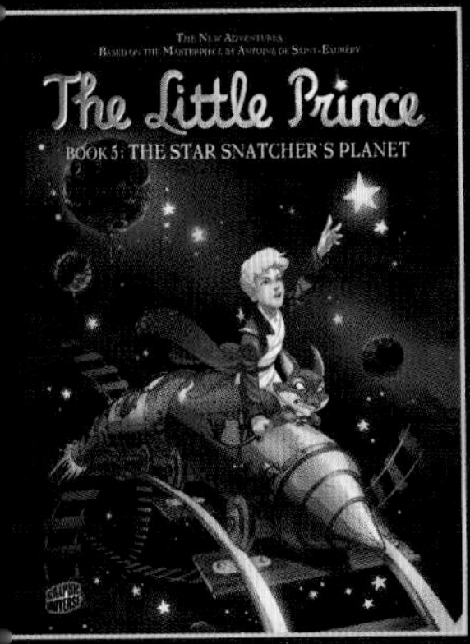
The Little Prince
BOOK 5: THE STAR SNATCHER'S PLANET
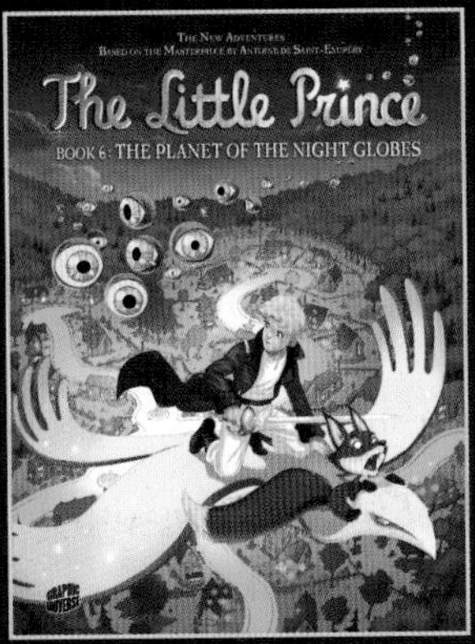
The Little Prince
BOOK 6: THE PLANET OF THE NIGHT GLOBES
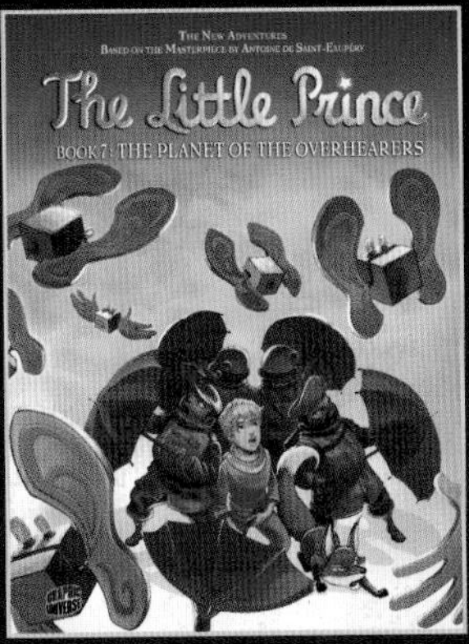
The Little Prince
BOOK 7: THE PLANET OF THE OVERHEARERS
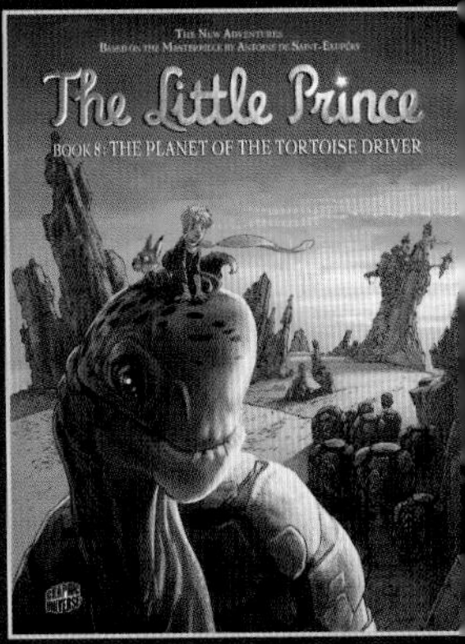
The Little Prince
BOOK 8: THE PLANET OF THE TORTOISE DRIVER

Book 1: The Planet of Wind

Book 2: The Planet of the Firebird

Book 3: The Planet of Music

Book 4: The Planet of Jade

Book 5: The Star Snatcher's Planet

Book 6: The Planet of the Night Globes

Book 7: The Planet of the Overhearers

Book 8: The Planet of the Tortoise Driver

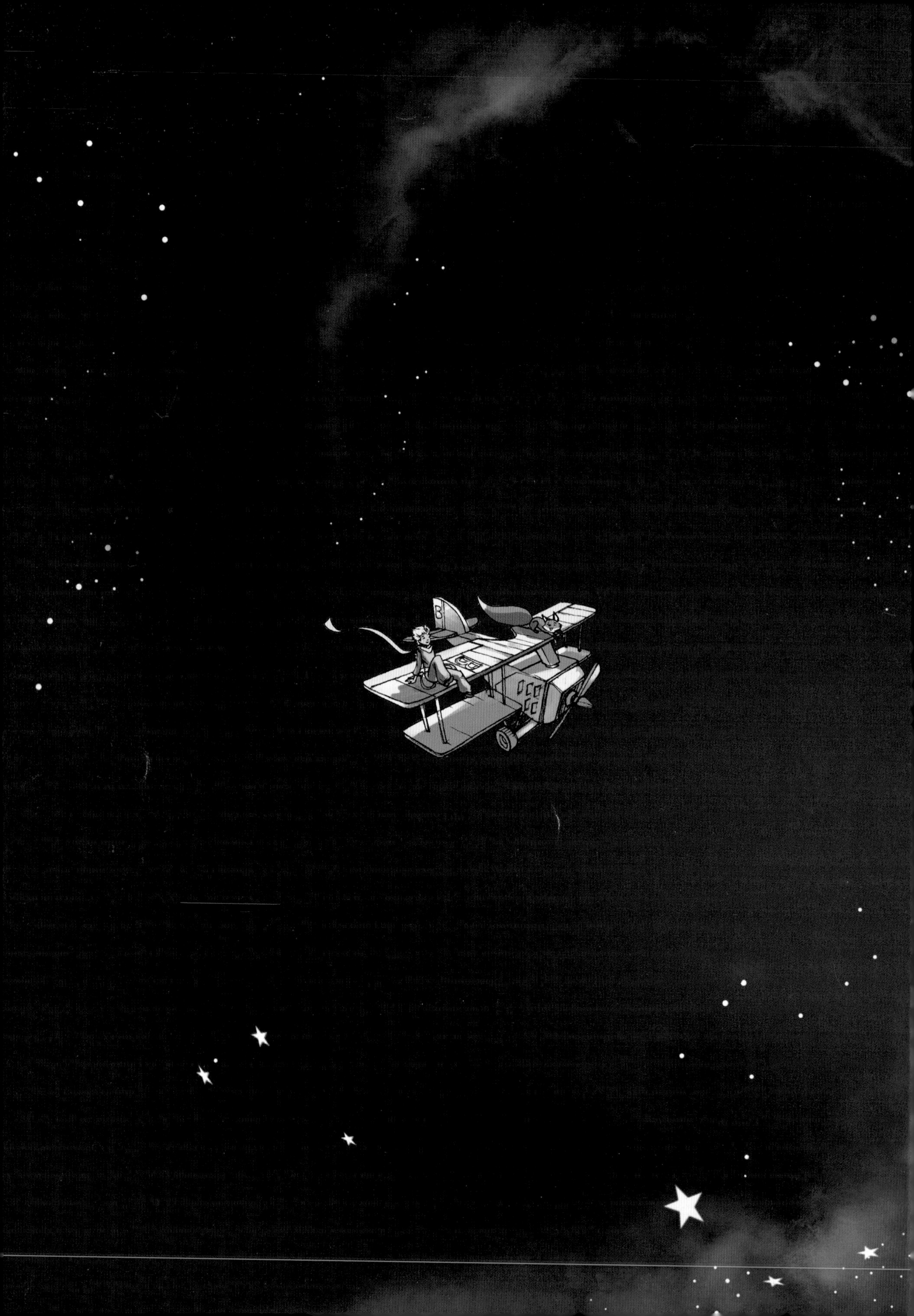